'My mother's not here, Dr McPherson.'

'I haven't come to see your mother.' Sinclair's voice was casual as he brushed past her.

Scarlet willed herself to relax and perched on the settee furthest away from him. 'Your visit is inappropriate. I'm a married woman.'

'Are you?'

Her heart thumped and she shot a look at him. 'What did you say?'

'Did your mother mention I spent some time with Cameron?' Sinclair asked.

Scarlet's heart thumped again. 'In passing she did.' She swallowed a lump in her throat. 'So?'

Sinclair stared back at her blandly. 'He's a fine boy. Don't you think he's handsome? Like me?'

'Cameron?' Her  couldn't think of like his father.'

Fiona McArthur is Australian and lives with her husband and five sons on the mid-north coast of New South Wales. Her interests are writing, reading, playing tennis, e-mail and discovering the fun of computers—of course that's when she's not watching the boys play competition cricket, football or tennis. She loves her work as part-time midwife in a country hospital, facilitates antenatal classes and enjoys the company of young mothers in a teenage pregnancy group.

Fiona McArthur's web page can be viewed at: www.fionamcarthur.com

Recent titles by the same author:

FATHER IN SECRET
MIDWIFE UNDER FIRE!
DELIVERING LOVE

THE MIDWIFE'S SECRET

BY

FIONA McARTHUR

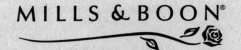

TO MY MOTHER THE ADVENTURER—
WITH ALL MY LOVE

First published in Great Britain 2002
Harlequin Mills & Boon Limited,
Eton House, 18-24 Paradise Road, Richmond, Surrey TW9 1SR

© Fiona McArthur 2002

ISBN 0 263 83081 0

Set in Times Roman 10½ on 12 pt.
03-0702-47001

Printed and bound in Spain
by Litografia Rosés, S.A., Barcelona

PROLOGUE

DR SINCLAIR MCPHERSON glanced down into the smoky depths of the bar with a grimace.

Wine bar nightlife was something he didn't often make the effort to investigate, but he had to stay over for the next day's medical presentation anyway.

He should have driven back to Southside. One of the local obstetricians had made the music here sound promising, but Sinclair wasn't so sure he needed the lung cancer.

The bar was crowded and noisy when he descended and he almost returned to his motel television but then the music started up again.

The haunting wail of a lone saxophone infiltrated his irritation with gossamer fingers the way sirens pulled ships to the rocks. But the real siren was oblivious to his presence as she stood in the far corner under an overhead spotlight.

Her body swayed in a slinky red dress, while her glorious copper hair floated in a thick cloud around her head. He could feel the music vibrating in his veins and shook his head to break the spell. It didn't work. She seduced the saxophone and Sinclair with her eyes closed.

She seemed vaguely familiar, and his brow creased as he tried to place where he'd seen her, then he shrugged. She embodied every fantasy that he'd held of the perfect woman—and that made her an old friend.

Sinclair eased to the bottom of the stairs and leant on the rail to drink in the sound and sight of her. He couldn't look away, and even tried closing his eyes, but her image was still there, burning in his brain.

People pushed past him and he restrained the urge to tell the chatterers to shut up and listen.

When she finished the notes drifted away on the chatter and he sighed. The spell was broken.

His hand reconnected to his body and released his grip on the rail. Wryly, Sinclair shook the tingling out of his fingers as she stepped down from the stage.

Her smile was like sunlight in the dimness of the bar and she continued to sway to some inner beat as she moved towards a boisterous table at the side of the room. Unable to stop himself, he cut through the crush towards her.

Unexpectedly, a drunken reveller's hand landed on her shoulder to detain her and Sinclair's response to the sight surged up irresistibly like a kick in the gut. Close enough, he stepped forward and between them so that the wine-saturated breath of the drunk blew in his face instead of hers. One hundred per cent alcoholic garlic. Sinclair coughed and turned his head to look down at her, his smile quizzical. 'Would you like this gentleman to leave you alone?'

Eyes wide and voice husky with confusion, she turned to him with relief. 'Yes, please.'

Sinclair glared into the unfocussed eyes below him. 'Sorry, friend. You're not welcome.' Even in his alcoholic haze the drunk backed off.

Sinclair watched the man stagger away for a moment before looking back at her. Then the vision laughed up at him and he felt the bands around his heart expand along with the silly smile on his face.

'A he-man? I haven't seen that side of you, Dr McPherson.' Her voice was deliciously playful and it was a moment before he realised she knew his name. Then, like a light switch flicking on inside his head, he knew where he'd seen her. She was one of the quieter midwives at Southside—Sister Robin—but he'd never seen a glimpse of this side of her.

Sinclair clamped his lips together to stop his mouth falling open. He probably saw the woman briefly several times a week but he couldn't remember a non-patient-related conversation with her.

'I'm sorry. Letty Robin, isn't it? I didn't recognise you.' Great comeback, McPherson, he chided himself. But she still had him stunned. He'd never have believed it. The mouse? He couldn't relate the painfully shy woman—well, he'd always assumed she was shy—with the vibrant vision in front of him.

'Scarlet, are you OK?' The rest of her party, more musicians or hippies by the look of them, surged around her. Sinclair allowed himself to be swept with them back to their table, still bemused by the strength of his reaction to someone he worked with. He strained his memory for the last time they'd spoken, and the only visual memories he could come up with seemed to be of him talking to the bun on the top of her head. He must have been asleep for the last few years. Maybe it was all a strange dream but he didn't want to bypass a second of it. He frowned. Why did they call her Scarlet?

He asked her once they'd sat down, her by his side. 'Letty is short for Scarlet and these friends have always called me that,' she shouted over the din. 'We've jammed together a long time, but not in public.' Her eyes sparkled with excitement. 'We've just made our own CD. The local music shop has sold a whole six copies.'

He grinned back at her delight. 'That's an occasion.'

'It's also my birthday, and tonight they arranged for me to play in public to get the feel of it.'

'Happy birthday. So how did it feel to be up there?' He couldn't look away as she swallowed what looked like apple cider in a soothing draught and relaxed back in the chair.

Her lips were soft and shiny and eminently kissable. He felt like picking up her glass and pressing his own lips to the spot where her mouth had been. Or, better still, those lips. Then she spoke again and he dragged his gaze back to her eyes.

'Performing live is scary. And not something I want to do on a regular basis. But I'm breaking out tonight.' She smiled that broad-daylight sunbeam right at him and for the first time he wished he could play a musical instrument or at least sing a note so he'd have something in common with her.

Until he realised he did have something in common with her. He worked with the woman. He couldn't believe he'd never felt the pull of attraction to her before. Pull? He felt like a bullock team was dragging him along.

He wanted to see that smile again. 'My voice makes a dog howl.'

She grinned at him and then one of the others at the table drew her attention and Sinclair sat back and just watched her. In this company she was vivacious and witty and vibrantly alive. He'd never seen her like that at work. It was still difficult to fathom but, then, he'd always been at the centre of the crowd and at work the more outgoing staff, and more lately, Tessa, tended to take over the conversations.

The motel's television was long forgotten as he bought her another cider and chatted with her friends, his eyes always searching for her smile.

When he finally managed to secure a dance with her, he realised what had been missing all the years he'd danced before. The soft material of her dress shifted seductively beneath his fingers and their bodies swayed together perfectly. Scarlet against him was a whole new way of dancing.

Reality receded even further as she leant into his shoulder and he smoothed the fabric. 'I love your dress,' he murmured.

She twirled in his arms and laughed up at him. 'A present to myself on my twenty-fifth birthday. Wicked, eh?'

'As sin,' he said huskily and pulled her closer into his arms. Scarlet filled his senses like a potent wine yet there was an air of innocence about her that baffled him.

The time raced away and when her friends left to go home he looked at the clock with indecision. He felt like a randy sixteen-year-old and just as unsure of himself. He couldn't let her go yet.

'I don't want this evening to end, Scarlet. Stay with me.' He gazed down at her and her eyes were like blazing jewels in her face, almost glittering as she stared up at him. Then she laughed and swept up her bag and her saxophone case.

'Let's make a night of it we'll never forget then, Sinclair.'

*   *   *

When he woke in the morning, she was gone, as if she'd never been. Yet his body could still feel the pressure and pleasure of hers. He knew for a fact that she didn't make a habit of sleeping with strange men—so why would she leave? He ran his hand over the slight indent her head had made in the pillow beside his and caught a faint wisp of her flowery perfume on his fingers. His feeling of loss caused a lump of disquiet in his usually cast-iron stomach.

Later that afternoon, when he took the steps to Southside's Maternity Ward two at a time, Sinclair looked at the place with new eyes. Someone here would be able to give him Scarlet's address. Unfortunately, the first person he saw was Tessa, sitting alone at the desk.

'Sinclair? You're back early. I thought the conference went for another day?' The tall midwife's pleased smile reminded him and a twinge of guilt pulled a frown between his eyes. They'd been out for dinner a few times but he'd never promised Tessa anything. He knew now what he'd been waiting for.

'Something came up.' He watched her lift one sculptured eyebrow. Clinically, he could see her beauty, but she couldn't compare with the joy he found in Scarlet. It was only fair that Tessa knew that. Be honest with her, McPherson, he chided himself. 'Actually...someone...came up.' He couldn't help the smile that followed or the implication that his change of plans had been because of a woman.

Her face stilled and she looked away for a moment before turning back to him.

'I'm pleased for you. Anyone I know?'

Sinclair hesitated, an uneasy reluctance warring

with his desire for the information he wanted. He'd have to ask someone.

'You wouldn't have Letty Robin's home phone number and address, would you?'

'Letty Robin?' The eyebrows went up again in disbelief. 'My, my.'

Sinclair heard footsteps approaching down the corridor and frowned at her. 'That's enough.'

'Captured her heart, have you? I went to school with Letty—she's always been a funny, shy little thing. What a good catch for someone like her. I understand her father never acknowledged her. You do know her mother was unmarried?'

'No, I didn't.' If Tessa didn't shut up he'd strangle her. Sinclair's voice became very soft so only she could hear him. 'I hope you're not going to play the woman scorned, Tessa.'

Tessa stood up and draped her arm around his shoulders before whispering in his ear.

'Me? Scorned? Never.' Then her voice returned to normal. 'I know you'll come back to me.' She moved away from him around the desk and her lips curved in a smile of greeting as someone he didn't see left through the front door.

He ignored Tessa's conceit, too immersed in his own world to take notice of her. 'Address, please.'

'The staff book is on the shelf—she lives in the nurses' home.' Tessa laughed and he squashed the feeling of disquiet that grew with her smile. Lord, save him from all women—bar one.

As she walked down the steps of Maternity, Scarlet's face felt frozen. There were a lot of reasons she regretted the night she'd spent with Sinclair McPherson.

And conversations like the fraction she'd just overheard between Sinclair and Tessa only emphasised her regret.

She'd hoped she'd grown out of her inferiority complex about her birth but hearing Tessa's snide comments to Sinclair took Scarlet back to her schooldays. The last five years had been peaceful until Tessa had resettled in Southside a few months ago.

She needed to get away and think this thing through, Scarlet realised. She'd been a fool last night and it was the lack of any future in it that was the worst. But when Sinclair had looked at her finally, with all the admiration she'd ever dreamed of, she'd felt beautiful and worthy of him.

A one-night stand with a man she'd fancied for years. How stupid could she get? His eyes had been on Tessa since she came back and from the way she'd been draped all over him, whispering sweet nothings in his ear, it seemed like they were right back where they belonged at this moment.

Scarlet had watched him drifting into a relationship with her nemesis and she'd really thought she'd accepted the cruel fate that had spelt the end of any fanciful dreams she'd held. She just didn't have it in her to fight Tessa for him.

Then last night, drunk not on wine but on Sinclair's undivided attention, she had gone back to that motel with him. Knowing what she did and risking what she had, she'd weakly thrown away the self-esteem she'd painstakingly earned over the last five years.

Self-esteem and respectability might not seem difficult to most people, she thought bitterly, but when you'd had the loss of it rammed down your throat by a bunch of school bullies for years it assumed enormous importance.

Her love of midwifery had done a lot to repair the damage but obviously her own illegitimacy was something she still hadn't come to terms with. She had to get away.

Sinclair was frustrated, more so than he had ever been before in his life. Letty, or Scarlet as he now thought of her, was gone. She wasn't home, didn't answer her messages and didn't come to work. As suddenly as she'd entered his life she'd left it. Later in the week, when he questioned the charge nurse about the midwives' roster, he was told that Letty was on leave for two weeks. Then it had been extended to twelve months. Her nurses' home room was deserted. Eventually one of the other midwives mentioned a phone call from her about a whirlwind courtship with some geologist up in the hills and that she was married!

CHAPTER ONE

LATE in August, Sinclair McPherson, Director of Obstetrics at Southside, rubbed the bristles on his chin, unaware his life was about to change again.

Four o'clock in the morning was too early to shave, he defended himself, not breaking stride down the hallway.

He glanced up at the 'birth imminent' red light that glowed gently outside Labour Ward One, knocked briefly and stepped around the door into the room.

He frowned, momentarily confused. The labour ward bed was empty and there seemed to be an inordinate number of women present at first glance. Then he realised the birthing woman was kneeling on a mat at the side of the room. He sighed.

Times were changing. Still, the good news was that it seemed he'd made it with a few minutes to spare to be present for the birth. Surely she'd hop onto the bed at the last minute. A natural, uncomplicated birth was always a pleasure, even at this time of the morning.

The woman he'd been called to see—Mrs Connors—was earthily naked and he could hear the tiny puffs as she pushed gently with the contraction. He couldn't remember seeing her name antenatally, so she must have visited one of the other practitioners. He shrugged. It wasn't uncommon to meet a woman for the first time in labour if you covered as many calls as he did.

A cascade of deep copper hair screened her face and there was something beautifully primal about her that touched him. He shook his head at the unusual thought.

In fact, the whole room had a peacefulness that wasn't common at this time. Sinclair opened his mouth to speak and then decided against it. She was too busy for him to introduce himself at this moment. He heard the longer exhalation of her breath as he made his way to the sink where he began to wash his hands and gown up as usual.

'Get him out of here!' The woman's words were strong and clear and vehement with intent.

Sinclair froze and turned back towards the group huddled around the woman on the floor. He reached for the towel and bit back a sigh. Hormones. Women in labour were known to be irrational at times and he'd taken his fair share of abuse over the years. He smiled slightly. They usually apologised profusely once their babies were born.

A tall woman, probably her mother, Sinclair guessed, brushed the sweep of thick hair off her daughter's face. She soothed her. 'It's OK, Scarlet.'

Sinclair looked into his patient's face for the first time, recognition hitting him like a freight train. He squeezed the towel between his fingers.

Here, in the final throes of labour, were the delicate cheekbones and luminous eyes that had haunted his thoughts.

Now, only the second time he'd seen her beautiful hair loose from its usual bun, she was in labour!

'Scarlet—I mean Letty?' Sinclair was unaware of the speculative glances the others in the room cast his way at his use of her birth name.

When she'd been a midwife here, her actions had always been controlled, and she'd never raised her voice above a low murmur. But that night, and now in the throes of childbirth, it was as if someone had turned a light on. Her strength and vitality shimmered from her.

Don't go there, he warned himself, and dragged his mind away from the memories.

Another breath whooshed between her lips but there was no problem understanding her next words. 'I *said* get him out. He's the last person I want here.'

This was ridiculous. Sinclair quelled the flicker of pain her request caused. 'I'm here to help you, Letty.' He tried to establish his role as doctor and benign father figure. 'It will all be over soon.'

Her look seared him with scorn. 'I know that,' she said and her gasp, as a new wave of pain engulfed her, made him wince. She looked away from him, to some hidden place, to concentrate on the progression of the baby's head. Then she sighed again as the contraction ebbed. 'This is all your fault.'

Sinclair's heart skipped a beat and then galloped off in a bolt. Surely not? She would have told him. November, December, January… It was late August now… Sinclair's usually analytical brain scrambled as he tried to work it out. No. He'd used protection.

He shook his head. He was inferring too much here. 'All right, Letty. I know it hurts.' He forced the next words. 'But I'm sure your *husband*—' he couldn't help the hardness he injected into the word 'husband' '—is more at fault than I. Now, perhaps you could let me see where you are up to.'

She gave a slightly hysterical laugh and then gritted

her teeth. 'The midwife will deliver my baby. Please, leave—before I say something I'll really regret.'

Now he could feel the hostility from the other women in the room. He glanced at Michelle, the midwife in charge, and she shrugged wryly as if to apologise for calling him.

'Fine.' He erased all expression from his face. 'I'll be outside in the corridor if you need me.'

The sound of the door as he pulled it shut coincided with the unmistakable sounds of the last moments before birth. Then he heard a baby's cry and the murmur of congratulatory voices.

Sinclair pushed himself off the door. He felt as if someone had burst a large paper bag in his face. What the hell had that been about? But most disturbing of all—Scarlet was back. With a baby!

Scarlet Robin sank back in the bed and clasped her new son skin to skin against her breast. He snuffled to match her own ragged breath and she realised at last the wait was over. 'I'll call him Cameron.'

A great wave of love for the infant lying against her took her by surprise, and she brushed her lips across his damp hair. She'd done it. Scarlet caught the tears in her mother's eye.

'Thanks for your help, Mum.'

'Congratulations, darling. Welcome to motherhood,' Vivienne said.

Scarlet smiled and glanced at two other women, both dressed in brightly tie-dyed sarongs. 'And thanks, both of you, for bringing me in from the valley and down the mountain. You made me strong with your presence.'

The younger of the two was heavily pregnant and

ran her hand nervously over her bulging stomach. 'You were wonderful, Scarlet. And you were right. It wasn't so bad at the hospital.'

Scarlet relaxed back against the beanbag. 'Good girl, Leah. At least you'll have some idea what it's like here, just in case.'

Leah glanced guiltily at her friend. 'I'm sure I'll be fine with Crystal at the community.'

The other woman, long-faced and expressionless, nudged her. 'We'd better go and leave Scarlet with her new son. It was interesting, seeing the hospital side.'

Leah nodded and her long plaits swung around her face. 'Bye, Cameron. Bye, Vivienne.' She smiled shyly at the hospital midwife. 'And you, too, Michelle.' As they left, Crystal said nothing.

Michelle waved and followed them to the door to shut it after them. 'Is Leah having her baby in the valley?'

'Baby is breech at the moment and she's hoping it will turn before labour. But she's promised she'll come here if it doesn't.' Scarlet ran her finger down the incredible softness of her baby's leg.

'Who's the other woman?' Michelle's voice made Scarlet look up.

'Crystal is the new valley midwife, she's determined Leah will have her baby at the community.'

Michelle raised her eyebrows. 'I noticed a bit of attitude.' The other midwife slid the blood-pressure cuff over Scarlet's arm and pumped it up. Stethoscope in ears, she asked the question that Scarlet knew had been burning to get out. 'So what was all that business with Dr McPherson?'

Scarlet glanced pointedly at her constricted arm.

'Um, Michelle? Could you let the air out? Otherwise my arm will drop off.' The slow hiss of deflation made them both smile.

The few seconds gave Scarlet time to formulate an answer. 'It was nothing personal. A tirade against men. You know what women in labour are like. Forget it.' She glimpsed her mother's raised eyebrows and frowned her to silence.

Cameron chose that moment to make his presence heard and the women all hustled to pacify him. Within moments he nursed quietly at his mother's breast with a warm blanket tucked securely around them both.

Michelle stepped back. 'He's got the hang of it. I'm off to empty my trolleys before we get you show-ered. Press your call button if you need me. It's great to see you back. Congratulations, Letty. Or should I call you Scarlet?' she teased.

'Whatever strikes your fancy.' Scarlet gave a wry smile and shook her head. 'I'm not sure who I am at the moment. Thanks anyway and I'll call you if I do need help.'

That left three generations of the Robin family alone in the room, and the silence lengthened between mother and daughter.

Finally Vivienne could stand it no longer. 'So what are you going to do about his surname on the birth certificate? Are you going to call him Connors after your absent husband, Robin after you or…' Vivienne paused and squeezed her daughter's hand '…perhaps McPherson after his father?'

Scarlet refused to meet her mother's eyes. 'What's Sinclair McPherson got to do with this?' But her voice lacked conviction.

Her mother raised her eyebrows. 'I've had my suspicions and the reactions of both of you today confirmed it. I really couldn't swallow the travelling-geologist-husband story. I'm sorry, darling.'

Scarlet raised her own eyebrows, not realising how much she resembled her forthright mother when she did so.

Then she sighed. 'It was my fault for weakening when Sinclair turned up at the nightclub. Just one let-my-hair-down vulnerable moment and the last five years here, spent trying to be perfect, were wasted.'

Vivienne shook her head. 'Well, stop trying to be perfect. I never liked you shortening your name to Letty. Scarlet is a strong name. Blaze a trail and be yourself.'

Scarlet narrowed her eyes. 'I always knew he was dangerous.'

'Did you, now?' Vivienne bit back a smile. 'I wonder why that is?'

Scarlet was too immersed in her own problems to notice. 'I'd hoped by creating Mr Connors I could protect my child from the rumours.' And me from Sinclair. But she didn't say it. She looked up at her mother. 'It seemed like a good idea at the time.'

Vivienne sighed. 'I can't help feeling you'd be better to face the gossips and be done with it.'

Scarlet sank back in the bed. 'Of course you do. You called me Scarlet. I've worn my illegitimacy branded on my forehead all my life. I won't have that for my son. I like being unobtrusive Letty, and it feels like I've spent the last twenty-five years avoiding scandal like the plague. It's so pathetic that one mad loss of control ruined it all.'

'I'm sorry you feel that way, Scarlet.' Vivienne bit

her lip. 'But I think you'd find that you're the only person who can read the writing you're so sure is there. Sinclair may even surprise you and I believe he should have the chance.'

Scarlet watched her mother stand up from the bed and stroke her new grandson's cheek. 'At least you came back to have him here. I'm grateful for that,' she said. Vivienne picked up her bag from the side bench. 'I should have minded my own business. I'll see you later this morning. Try and get some rest.' Scarlet watched her mother blow a kiss and leave.

Scarlet sighed and closed her eyes. She hadn't meant to hurt her mother. She'd felt more attuned to her in the last twelve hours than she ever had. Maybe Vivienne did understand what she was going through? This was probably the first time she'd let Vivienne get really close to her. Now that was an unattractive thought. Had she really been that obsessed with her own problems?

Cameron had settled to infrequent sucks and Scarlet knew she should detach and burp him to protect her nipples from damage. She slid the tip of her little finger into the side of his mouth and broke the suction—just as she had shown the technique to countless new mothers.

It was strange, being the mother and not the midwife.

A lot of the assurance she'd shown as adviser to inexperienced mums seemed to have slipped away somewhere. Now she held this child who was totally her responsibility, she could feel the fear of doing the wrong thing threaten to overwhelm her. Was this how all mothers felt—or just those who were parenting on their own? She cupped his tiny foot in her hands and watched his toes spread at the sensation.

She wished there were someone there she could share her delight with as she smiled over his perfect tiny feet. Which brought her back to Sinclair.

What about Sinclair? Should she have told him? Given him a chance? Was her mother right to advise her to brazen it out? The problem was, she wasn't the brazen-it-out type. Not like her mother.

And when Sinclair married someone else, as he would one day, would that woman's children bully Cameron like she'd been bullied?

Scarlet shook her head. She couldn't face it. She imagined the furore if Scarlet Robin named the town's most eligible bachelor as the father of her child. She shuddered.

Then there was Tessa. How ironic that the taunting child of her schooldays was practically engaged to the only man she'd ever slept with. Now there would be another illegitimate child for Tessa's children to taunt. But even more ironic was the fact that the person who had undermined Scarlet's confidence for so long was her half-sister. Only Tessa would never know that.

A wave of fierce protectiveness for Cameron rose in her heart. Nobody would victimise her son. This way Scarlet Connors would be a respectable married woman and Cameron would be like every other child. She'd never shared with her mother how virulent the jibes had been right through her school years until a wall of suppressed emotion had blocked true communication between mother and daughter.

And this morning, when Sinclair had walked in, she'd nearly blown it at the last moment.

With his presence in the labour room she'd felt her

control slipping through her fingers like silk through a loop. What she'd lost, what might have been—it had all been there for distraction at a time that hadn't permitted distractions.

In a perfect world, he would have been beside her to grip her hand for the last twelve hours, to wipe her brow and moisten her mouth as she'd struggled and strained and finally exulted in the birth of their child.

But it had been a mockery to see him enter a few moments before the end. To see the glory and not the journey it had taken to get there. Instead, he'd stood tall and straight, in his work suit and tie, every inch the distinguished country specialist, here to 'attend' another birth.

It was hard to imagine the two of them so lost to sense and reason that Cameron could have been conceived.

She shook her head at the memory. Sinclair's fleeting touch leading to a whisper of a kiss, leading to the first sign of the impending storm.

But lightning was like that.

A cataclysmic mating of passing storms—wild winds of passion interspersed with miraculous rainbows of joy—but even the most perfect storm had to end.

She could remember lingering the next morning, despite the shock of what they'd done, to catch a last sight of him with his dark hair tousled on the motel room pillow. His ridiculously long lashes had rested on his cheeks as she'd slipped away. It had been then that she'd known that she couldn't face him without the world finding out how she felt. Or face the fact he'd never be hers. She'd needed to get away—from

Sinclair and what she'd done—just for a week or two to come to grips with her own weakness.

The nurse manager had been baffled but understanding over her sudden need for a short leave of absence. Then Scarlet had found out about her pregnancy and she'd extended it to twelve months.

The strange thing was, even though the last nine months spent at the valley community had been special, Scarlet had never felt tempted to have her baby anywhere else but here at Southside. She must be a masochist.

Hopefully, Gerry the geologist—she grimaced wryly at the alliteration she jogged her memory with—her fictitious husband, would protect her son. She really must get her story straight.

With more luck, now Cameron was born, she wouldn't be as scatterbrained as she'd felt during pregnancy. She had to remember to tell people he was in New Guinea—or was that New Hebrides? Or should she just kill him off? Ditch him? Her eyes closed. It was all too hard at the moment and she dozed with her son as the sky turned pink in a beautiful dawn.

'How are you now, Mrs Connors?' Sinclair stressed the 'Mrs' but Scarlet wasn't sure if it was for her sake or for Tessa standing beside him as he did his ward rounds.

She could feel herself turn back into inconspicuous Letty as he towered over her, and she frowned. Why would that annoy her? Wasn't that what she wanted?

She looked down at the sheet crumpled between her fingers and smoothed it. 'I'm fine, thank you. I must apologise for my rudeness in the labour ward this morning, Dr McPherson.' She looked up and caught a brief flash of emotion cross his face before he schooled his expression.

'Not a problem.' He stepped forward to the little cot and peered in at her baby. 'What are you calling him?'

Scarlet couldn't help comparing Cameron's naming process to the usual father-mother discussion. 'I've called him Cameron.'

'A good strong name,' he said, and untucked the baby sheet. 'I'll do a newborn check on this fellow now, too, as I missed doing it at his birth.' He turned to the midwife. 'Perhaps you could find me one of those infant stethoscopes from the nursery, please, Tessa?'

Scarlet suppressed a wince at the glowing smile Tessa bestowed on Sinclair as she hurried to do his bidding. Some things never changed. He'd always been everyone's grey-eyed boy and then favorite man—even Scarlet's. He'd never noticed her and she hadn't pushed it, as if she'd sensed how easily he could have broken her heart if he had. It had been safer hiding in full view—as dull and dutiful Letty.

She looked from baby to father. Earlier, Scarlet had been sure that he had his father's determined chin and beautiful mouth. Now she found herself searching Sinclair's face for other signs of paternity. Or was she filling a need to drink in the sight of the man who affected her so deeply?

Affected her so profoundly that she'd run.

A headlong flight that had meant leaving Southside where she'd finally carved a comfortable niche for herself—until, of course, Tessa had moved home—in a profession she adored. A need to leave rather than face a loss of control that had rocked the foundations of the safe life she'd built for herself.

Now she had come to terms with what she wanted out of life. She still believed she had done the right thing. It had been time to come home.

Sinclair's black hair was slightly shorter than she remembered and his face seemed thinner. Those straight brows were drawn together as he competently undressed and examined Cameron for any signs of abnormality. His intense concentration made his cheekbones more prominent, and her fingers itched to run down the side of his face as she remembered doing that night. She must have been mad.

His sudden stillness warned her and she glanced away from his face to his hands. He'd turned Cameron over to run his finger down his spine and he'd seen the small dark brown mole glistening on the baby's buttock like a tiny brown paint spill.

Sinclair lifted his head and stared at her. She could tell his mind was racing and a cold fear clutched at her stomach. She moistened her lips and strove for a calm voice. Those birthmarks were quite common.

'I saw that this morning. Apparently my father had one.'

He answered almost absently as if his mind was still elsewhere. 'It's a congenital melanocytic naevus. They occur when melanocytes, the cells which produce skin pigmentation, accumulate in large numbers, producing a dark patch of skin. Usually greater than one centimetre in size, it's basically a mole that tends to run in families.'

'That was impressive.' Scarlet couldn't keep the tinge of sarcasm out of her voice. 'Obviously you've seen them before.' This wasn't an interesting case they were talking about. This was her baby!

Sinclair's beautiful grey eyes narrowed and a grim smile played across his lips. 'Yes, I've seen them before. Both my father and I have one, and we're fine.'

Tessa swept in with the stethoscope and Sinclair looked back at Cameron as he held out his hand.

Scarlet sagged unobtrusively against the pillows and resisted the urge to clutch her chest. That wasn't proof. She was being foolish. He'd said 'tends to run in families'—not *always* run in families. He didn't suspect anything. She hoped.

The examination was soon over and Sinclair stepped back for Tessa to re-dress the baby. Cameron's indignant cries filled the room.

Scarlet curled her fingers and resisted the urge to snatch him from the other woman and dress him herself. It was only a moment later before she had him safe in her arms but it was illuminating. So this was how new mothers felt!

That was another basketful of empathy she would have when she came back to work.

Sinclair wrote in Cameron's newborn health book and slipped it back under the cot. 'Everything seems OK. Cameron is a fine healthy baby. So when does his father get to see him?'

Scarlet jumped and her mind went blank. 'I'm sorry?'

Sinclair's gaze drilled into hers and she sat, transfixed like a rabbit caught in headlights on the road. 'Your husband? I believe he's overseas at present and couldn't be here for Cameron's birth.'

Right. 'Of course. In New Hebrides.' Scarlet

stretched a smile across her frozen face. 'I'm not sure, but he was thrilled when I spoke to him this morning.'

Sinclair smiled but his eyes were hard. 'I'm sure any man would be proud to have a son like Cameron. Have a restful day, Letty.' He nodded and gestured for Tessa to precede him from the room.

Scarlet felt sick. She had to get out of here before rounds the next day. Please, God, she would handle seeing Sinclair more easily when she wasn't so emotionally drained from labour.

On his way out of the hospital Sinclair's mind wasn't on where he walked and he almost bumped into Scarlet's mother as she entered through Reception. She was taller than her daughter or perhaps it was just the way she carried herself.

But, then, he was beginning to wonder if that depended on whether the young woman in question was playing Letty or Scarlet.

'Good morning, Mrs Robin.'

'Good morning, Dr McPherson. And it's Miss Robin not Mrs.'

Sinclair blinked but recovered quickly. He could feel a small smile tug at the corner of his mouth. 'Miss Robin.' He inclined his head. 'I've just checked your new grandson over. He's a fine young lad.'

Vivienne smiled. 'Ten fingers and toes, I assume. He'd better have. Scarlet couldn't have tried any harder to be healthy.'

'Just the congenital melanocytic naevus on his buttock. Any family history you know of for that?'

'Come again?' Vivienne's brow wrinkled.

Sinclair grinned self-mockingly. 'Sorry, brown mole.'

The older woman raised one arched eyebrow and gave her own small smile. 'Not that I'm aware of, but perhaps Scarlet will know. I haven't met her husband's family. Have a good day, Doctor.'

'Please, call me Sinclair.' He shrugged and shook his head. 'I feel like I've known you for a long time.' He could have sworn she looked startled.

'Funny, that. I'm Vivienne. I'll see you later, then, Sinclair.' She moved on, head high and no backward glance.

He continued on his way but the tension in his shoulders ached for release. Why had Scarlet/Letty lied about the mole unless she had a reason? Was he just being paranoid? Or was Scarlet hiding something? Like he had a son!

Hell. He'd finally started to get his life back together since she'd crashed into his world like a destructive comet and had left just as quickly. He'd been out again with Tessa a few times since then—and been congratulating himself on his good sense at returning to normality. He'd even started to think of those grandchildren his father kept asking for. Until this morning.

Once he'd seen Scarlet again, he'd had a hard time resisting the urge to return to the hospital to interrogate her. He'd probably worn a path in his carpet as he'd waited for normal round time because he hadn't trusted himself to see her that first time alone.

But he was no nearer the truth of why she'd disappeared than he'd ever been. And now it was too late.

At the thought of that magical night, his hand slid up to rub his neck and he dug his fingers into the knot of tension there. He couldn't believe how she'd affected him or how he'd behaved. That he, who'd never lost control before—or immersed himself in someone until the outside world had disappeared—had been so powerless to resist a woman.

His only hold on sanity had been the fact he'd used protection when they'd made love. Almost infallible.

But it must have been very shortly after their night together that she'd met her husband. An idea that didn't bear thinking about froze his steps. If Cameron was his own son, had he, Sinclair, forced her into a marriage she hadn't wanted and was now stuck in—because of the consequences of that night?

Surely not. She would have told him. Sinclair started walking again. And if that had been the case he would have married her himself! That stopped him cold.

Sinclair realised now he hadn't come to grips with the fact that Scarlet had disappeared before he'd even been able to attempt to repeat the experience of making love with her. Could he really consider spending the rest of his life with a woman he barely knew—not counting the little he'd seen of her at work?

When he'd received the news she'd married some geologist, the depth of his dismay had been a sobering realisation.

As the months had passed, the whole incident had become even more illusional until he'd almost convinced himself it had been a dream—a warning to be careful.

Well, that little indulgence had certainly come home to roost. It was a nightmare.

CHAPTER TWO

'I SAW Sinclair on my way in.' Vivienne placed the small blue-wrapped present on the bedside locker before she reached over to kiss her daughter on the forehead.

'Yes, he checked Cameron over.' Scarlet tried a smile but her face felt stiff. 'Mum, I want to go home. Today. You said we could move in with you.' She realised she was twisting the sheet again and stopped.

'Of course I'd love to have both of you.' Vivienne pulled the chair up beside the bed. 'I never understood why you lived in the nurses' home all those years. But why today?'

Scarlet met her mother's eyes. 'I'd feel more relaxed away from here.'

'Away from Sinclair, you mean.' It was a statement not a question. Vivienne frowned.

Scarlet sank back against the pillows. 'It doesn't matter what the reason is. Take us home, please.'

'If that's what you want.' Vivienne patted her hand. 'Give me time to make a few preparations and if it's OK with your doctor, I'll pick you up this afternoon. I must take home those bags the girls brought in with you. You said one had the baby things in there?'

'Everything's there.' She pointed to three cases beside the bed. 'Thanks, Mum.' She kissed her son's head. 'We'll go home to Nana's, OK, darling?'

Vivienne mock shuddered. 'Don't you dare teach your child to call me Nana! Vivienne, please.'

* * *

The McPherson Family Practice was run from the front of what used to be four units overlooking the river. Sinclair had purchased and restored the outside of the block to its 1950's grandeur on his return from Sydney five years ago. Inside, renovations had converted the top floor and rear of the ground floor to spacious living accommodation with wonderful breezes and views.

This year he'd finally convinced his father to move in so they could see more of each other. Privately, Sinclair was concerned about his father's health.

The phone rang as Sinclair was about to go through to his consulting rooms. He listened, frowned at the news and then replaced the phone gently in the cradle afterwards. So Scarlet wanted to go home. Already? Funny how he now thought of her as Scarlet and not Letty. Was she trying to avoid seeing him or was her sudden wish for discharge for another reason altogether? He laughed self-mockingly. As if he understood her.

Of course, she could do what she liked and he couldn't stop her. But he had to see her once, alone, to settle what had been between them or he would go crazy.

He wished her bloody husband would come back, covered in naevi—the thought made him smile at the mental picture—so he could stamp on those suspicions that wouldn't leave his mind. The timing of Cameron's birth was too close for comfort but the real problem was that he couldn't get Scarlet out of his mind. He had to remember she was a married woman and out of his reach. Technically he shouldn't see her.

He heard the front door open and he followed the

sound of slow footsteps through to the kitchen. When he walked through, his father's shoulders had an unaccustomed droop to them. Sinclair frowned as the older man lowered himself heavily into a chair at the table.

'You OK, Dad?'

Dr Frank McPherson looked nearer to seventy than the sixty he was. 'Just in need of a holiday, my boy.' He looked up from under a tufted set of straight brows. 'I heard you go out in the early hours. Get there in time?'

'Technically.' There was that word again. Sinclair sat down at the table beside his father. He didn't want to elaborate on his eviction from the labour ward by his ex-lover.

'You deserve more than a holiday, Dad. You should be out having the time of your life now.'

His father ignored his son's not too subtle suggestion of retirement. 'What do you mean—technically?'

Sinclair sighed. 'Do you remember Letty Robin? She used to be a midwife from the hospital.'

'Daughter of Vivienne Robin?' A strange smile flitted across his lined face. 'Now, there's a woman. I haven't seen her for a while.'

Sinclair tilted his head. 'Is that a glint I see in your eye, Dad?'

'She's a dangerous woman. I almost lost my head over her—sometimes wish I had. I wonder if she's still got that fire that draws a man like a moth to a flame. I've never seen it in young Letty.' He glanced up at his son. 'But still waters run deep.'

'And I always thought you were pining for Mum.'

'Your mother was a good woman and didn't deserve to die young. We had a good marriage.' He changed the subject. 'Which reminds me! When are you going to provide me with some grandchildren?'

'Diversional tactics, Dad?' Sinclair couldn't help his thoughts going straight to Scarlet. He grimaced. 'I had hoped to give you a daughter-in-law before the children, if that's OK.'

'Well, mind I'm not dead before you do. So what's last night got to do with young Letty?'

'She had a son and I was called in.'

'Uncomplicated, I hope.' He didn't wait for an answer and had lost interest in the original question. 'So Vivienne's a grandparent before I am, eh?' His eyes twinkled and he stared off into the distance.

Sinclair tested the idea of saying there was some complication but not the type his father was talking about. He decided against it. That was between Scarlet and himself.

Scarlet heard her mother's doorbell ring just after six that evening. The murmur of voices didn't enlighten her and when Sinclair walked into the room she could only stare. Her breath caught and with her hand at her throat, she panicked for a moment. He seemed to fill the room from where she sat.

'Good evening, Scarlet.' His voice was calm and deep like she'd remembered, and it still activated the nerves all over her body. Would she ever be able to forget that night?

He was frowning at her. 'May I sit down?' He indicated the chair beside where she was sitting with Cameron.

She tried to crane her neck unobtrusively to see around him in case her mother was still available to rescue her, but his strong shoulders blocked any view of the hallway.

Sinclair's voice, at least, was amused. 'If you're looking for Vivienne, I asked her to give me a few moments alone with you.'

She straightened her head and nodded at the chair. When he sat down, he looked very relaxed as he crossed one well-shod foot over the other. Damn him. Scarlet licked dry lips and carefully met the cool grey of his eyes. 'Why are you here?'

'A little unfinished business.' The subtle undertones raised the hairs on her arms and she suppressed an urge to clasp Cameron closer to her chest.

She raised her chin. 'I'm sorry, I don't know what you mean, Dr McPherson.'

If anything, his eyes became cooler. 'I've handed your case to the women's health nurse to follow up. I thought you might be more comfortable. So I'm not here as your obstetrician. Please, call me Sinclair. You at least owe me that.'

At his words, her eyes flashed and she looked more like the Scarlet he remembered. 'I owe you nothing.' Then she looked away for a moment and when she looked back she still looked beautiful, with her copper hair loose around her shoulders. She also looked tired. He stifled the sudden urge to gather her in his arms and offer her a safe haven. Maybe he should leave her to rest?

He hardened his heart. She was married and this could be his last chance to talk to her alone. This was too important.

Her voice was flat when she went on, 'The Scarlet you met has gone. You caught me at a mad, vulnerable moment and totally out of character for me. I'm just plain old Letty whom you've walked past for years.'

He stared at her for a moment, and weighed her words. She'd never be plain anything to him again. But that wasn't her problem with a new husband and son. When he spoke, his voice was very quiet. 'I hope we can still be friends?'

Her startled gaze met his. 'I'm a married woman, Sinclair.'

Her voice lacked conviction and his pulse leapt with the subtle underlying implications. Did she already regret her marriage to this other man? Then she pressed on as if to cover her lack of fervour.

'And I'm a respectable mother who has come home for some peace and quiet until my husband comes back from New Guinea. And now, if you'll excuse me, I need my rest.'

He stood up and replayed her words in his mind. 'As you wish. I'll leave you to rest.' His final look was enigmatic. There was something not quite right here but he couldn't pinpoint it. 'My regards to your travelling husband—he certainly gets around.'

Scarlet stared after him and then heard the door close. Blast. She'd been rude and that wasn't like her. Why did Sinclair always do that to her?

Her brain felt scattered to the four corners of the earth. A bit like her absent husband who should have been in New Hebrides, not in New Guinea. She sighed but was too preoccupied with what Sinclair had said to care.

Sinclair McPherson wanted to be friends? What did that mean? He wanted an affair while her 'husband' was away? That thought was too big to contemplate even if there was some truth in it, which she couldn't believe, because if she did, she had a whole new set of problems.

The man could have any woman in Southside— why would he want her? She winced. Because she played good sax? She gave a strangled laugh. Good sex was more like it. Well, she'd learnt from the master. It was probably always that good for him.

She sighed and the tears scratched at the back of her throat. Cameron stirred in her arms and gave a little whimper. Grateful for the diversion, she lifted him over her shoulder to gently rub his back. He burped and the loud noise drew a smile from her.

'What a well-brought-up boy.' The oft-repeated phrase slipped out and the true meaning of it crashed in on her.

Her spine stiffened. Cameron would be well brought up. There would be no scandal attached to his name and the best way to achieve that was to remain in control. And that wasn't something she could guarantee if she let Sinclair McPherson into her orbit. Perhaps he was attracted to her, but lust wasn't love.

She was an unmarried mother and the daughter of an unmarried mother. Not exactly the perfect partner for the director of obstetrics at Southside Hospital. Especially if the truth came out that she'd fabricated a husband.

The only option was to remain in control of her life. Alone. Control was something she didn't seem to have much of when Sinclair was around.

'Are you OK, sweetheart?' Her mother broke into her thoughts and Scarlet looked up.

'I am now.' There was a new firmness in her voice.

She tightened her arms around Cameron. 'I'll be a mother my son will be proud of.'

'I never had any doubt of that, darling,' Vivienne said, her brow furrowed.

Scarlet sank her head back against the pillows of the lounge. That's it, then, she thought. 'I think I'll go to bed early.'

Vivienne hid her disappointment. 'It's only just dark.'

Her daughter gave an uneven laugh. 'At the community we slept and rose with the sun. No electricity there. I guess I'm used to it now. Sorry, Mum. I'll be better company tomorrow.'

Vivienne shrugged philosophically. 'You must think me a selfish old woman if you expect me to keep you up after the day you've had.'

'No. I know you have my best interests at heart.'

Two pairs of hazel eyes collided. 'Do you?'

'Goodnight, Mum.'

The first days blurred together and then a week had passed since Cameron's birth. Cameron demanded Scarlet's full attention for those early unsettled days, and all she seemed to do was feed him and sleep. Or lie in bed and think about Sinclair.

Another week passed and Cameron settled down to more regular feeds. But Scarlet couldn't seem to get her bounce back. She felt like she was living in a thick grey cloud.

Vivienne provided meals and support unobtrusively, and a new rapport began to build between mother and daughter.

Sinclair stayed away and Scarlet told herself she

was glad. The emptiness inside had to be because she was used to being busy.

'So, tell me what you did at the valley community. I imagined it's changed since I was there for your birth. We haven't had a chance to talk about it.' Vivienne was buttering her daughter's toast as Scarlet tried to eat breakfast and breastfeed at the same time.

'It's still very isolated from the world—utopia for the establishment haters—although they do have one mobile phone for emergencies. But the theme is still self-sufficiency and clean living.

'The majority of the food is grown there, as it was in the early days. Everyone made me very welcome when I turned up.' Scarlet remembered the moment when she'd decided that escape from Sinclair was harder than she thought. Until she'd remembered the commune where she'd been born.

Vivienne smiled. 'I remember when I arrived, too. Though there was only half a dozen families living there then. I'd just discovered I was pregnant with you and wanted to do everything right for the pregnancy.' Another piece of toast popped up in the toaster and Scarlet realised she'd eaten the last one already.

She accepted the new slice and smiled at her mother. 'We've never talked about it.'

'No. You haven't wanted to know.' Vivienne's voice was soft. 'But women change when they have their own baby. And we'll talk about it soon. Tell me about your time there.'

Scarlet stared at the food in her hand as she remembered. 'The previous midwife had just left and they were glad to see me. I took over the running of the clinic and ensured we had what was needed in first-aid supplies. But mostly I was the midwife. It's the same as when you lived there. Everyone has a task and certain responsibilities and it runs surprisingly smoothly.'

She smiled at the memory of her first couple of weeks. 'The maternity side was so different to the medicalised version of childbirth I was used to.' She shook her head. 'It was as if all the rules I had been taught had been ripped away. The true concept of midwifery in all its glory. But sometimes it was scary.

'These women didn't want me to deliver their babies—they wanted me ''with'' them while they did it themselves.' She laughed at the shock she had first battled with.

'It became the most incredible thrill to see them empowered by birth and not treated as *patients*.' She curled her lip over the word 'patients'.

Scarlet looked up to catch her mother staring at her.

Then Vivienne smiled. 'The time away has done you good. I've never seen you so passionate about anything before, except perhaps your music.'

Scarlet laughed, slightly embarrassed, and played with her toast. 'It certainly changed the way I feel about my role in childbirth. In fact, I think it actually changed me.' She looked up. 'I grew into being myself in the time I was there. There was no need for the rigid control I'd always thought essential when I worked at Southside.' But there was no Sinclair McPherson either, her thoughts mocked her. She pushed the disturbing concept away. 'I could be who I wanted and nobody thought any less of me.'

Vivienne shook her head. 'I've said that all along but you had other ideas. I admired your self-control but I could never understand it.'

'That's the joke. My self-control was important to my self-image. When I lost it with Sinclair I had to get away and see what was left of me to feel good about.' Scarlet laughed bitterly. 'And that was before I found out I was pregnant and the whole world was going to know how pathetic I was.'

Vivienne's eyes were suspiciously bright. 'Darling, I hate to hear you talk like that. If you feel that way because I didn't marry your father then I have a lot to answer for.' She met her daughter's eyes. 'Tessa's father would have married me, though I'd never tell his widow that.' A grim little smile hovered over her lips. 'But the man I should have married long before I met your father came back into my life and I wouldn't settle for second best. And except for your lack of a male role model as you grew up, and the fact that this is a small town, I don't regret that. Was your childhood so bad?'

Scarlet looked away and then her brows furrowed. She'd always believed her father hadn't wanted to marry the pregnant Vivienne. Scarlet thought of the few times she'd met the man she knew was her father accidentally in the street—unspoken conversations thick in the air between them. And her mother had refused him? She tamped down the hurt that he'd never wanted to know her. Well, it was his loss. Had her childhood been so bad? One day soon she would tell her mother about Tessa and her friends.

But here was something it didn't hurt to think about. Who was the other man? And how had she not known? 'Why didn't you marry the man you loved?'

Vivienne shrugged and stared down at the teacup in her hand. 'When his wife died, he didn't ask me and I was too proud to pursue him. Pride has a lot to answer for. But enough about me.' She offered to pour more tea and the subject was closed. 'Do you plan to resume at the hospital as a midwife or return to the valley?' The wistfulness in her voice was plain to both of them.

'Back to Southside—part time—as soon as I can.' Scarlet looked down at Cameron. 'My time at the valley is over. Crystal is the midwife now and in charge of the births. They don't need me.' Scarlet shrugged. 'Do you know that people come from all over New South Wales to spend the last few months of their pregnancies in the community because of the kind of births we have there?'

Vivienne patted her daughter's hand. 'It still sounds a wonderful place to be a part of—although I enjoy the creature comforts and the outside world myself.'

Scarlet nodded. 'For a time I thought I could stay for ever, but I must be a townie like you, Mum.' They both laughed. 'One of the good side issues about my time there was the opportunity to show that people who work in hospitals can be on the same wavelength as those in the valley community. I just hope I left the women with enough confidence that if they need to come to Southside for specialist care they'll rise above their reluctance. Or Crystal's reluctance.' She shook her head.

'It's something they haven't felt comfortable with, even in emergencies. I've promised to try and ensure their needs and choices will be respected. Hopefully, they'll realise that sometimes sick newborns will benefit from care that can't be provided in the valley.' She sipped the last of the tea and stared thoughtfully into the empty cup.

'That was the worrying part—no back-up if something did go wrong. Luckily it didn't in my time there. But I don't want to waste what I've learnt at the community.' She looked up at her mother and her eyes and voice showed the enthusiasm missing since she came home from hospital.

'I want to encourage change at Southside so that the women who choose to give birth there have the same chances as the community women to feel empowered by their births. It won't be easy but I'll fight for what I believe is their right.'

She grinned cheekily. 'I'm not sure how that's going to fit in with Southside doctors.'

Her mother sighed with relief. 'I love it when you're like this, Scarlet. I'm glad you're going back to Southside.'

Scarlet squeezed Vivienne's hand. 'The valley was a wonderful place to take time out from the world and have a healthy pregnancy, but I want Cameron to grow up able to hold his own in any setting.' She stroked his cheek and he stopped drinking for a moment to gaze into his mother's eyes.

'That's how I felt when it was time for you to start school,' Vivienne said.

Scarlet nudged her son under the chin and Cameron resumed his breakfast. 'He can visit when he's older, like when you took me back in my teens, but I've still got the money I saved before I left. I might buy my own house in town.'

'If that's what you want,' Vivienne said. 'But this house is too big for one person. It would be crazy to run two households.'

Scarlet searched her mother's face. 'I don't want to intrude. Cameron and I would make a huge change to your lifestyle.'

Vivienne laughed. 'No bigger than when you were born. I enjoy having you both. But it's up to you.' She stood up. 'They say mothers and daughters get on even better when the first grandchild hits the household.' She smiled down at her grandson.

'We missed out on a lot of that closeness when you were younger. I was so busy showing the world I didn't care what they thought, and you were tucked behind a wall I couldn't penetrate—maybe it's our time now. But that's enough soul-searching. Here...' She held out her hands. 'Give me my grandson and you go and shower. How do you feel about the three of us going to the shops today?' She smiled. 'Get us all out of the house.'

The shopping expedition was a disaster. Scarlet ran into three nursing friends who hadn't seen her since she'd left. She kept muddling her marriage story and Cameron grizzled as he picked up on his mother's tension.

Vivienne just smiled to herself as she ushered her daughter back to the car. 'The problem is, Scarlet, you're a terrible liar. Stick to "it didn't work out" and be done with it.'

'Making up a husband seemed like a good idea at the time.' Scarlet wiped a tense hand across her forehead.

'That's how most trouble starts. And here comes Dr McPherson.'

Scarlet's pulse rate jumped and she twisted her neck to search. 'Sinclair? Where?'

'Not Sinclair. Frank!' Vivienne smiled at the older man approaching and Scarlet felt like a fool as she recognised Sinclair's father. He was shorter than his son but one could see he'd been handsome when younger. And that he only had eyes for her mother.

'Hello, Vivienne. It's good to see you.' His greeting seemed unusually warm and Scarlet's forehead creased at the undercurrents between the older couple.

Even her mother's voice was softer than usual as she inclined her head. 'Frank, long time no see.' She turned towards Scarlet. 'You know my daughter, Scarlet?'

He smiled paternally at Scarlet and Cameron. 'I hear this chap dragged my son out of bed a couple of weeks ago.'

He smiled benignly down at Cameron and Scarlet hoped his son hadn't told him the full story.

He went on, 'Congratulations on your baby, young woman. He's a fine-looking lad.'

'I've recently acquired a son-in-law and a grandson,' Vivienne said. 'Scarlet's home with me while her husband's overseas.' She moved onto a new topic before he could comment. 'I hear you moved in with your son, Frank? No more wild parties for you.'

'I haven't a wild bone in my body, Vivienne. As well you know. It's at times like this that I regret it but I'm too old now.'

Scarlet looked from one to the other, feeling the conversation was on another level. The couple were oblivious to her presence and Cameron started to fuss. She stepped away to unlock the car and let the cool air in.

As she slid Cameron into his car capsule, she heard her mother say, 'We're not spring chickens any more but I don't like to hear you talk like that, Frank. Why don't you drop around for sherry this evening? We could catch up on old times or maybe play Scrabble.'

Scarlet heard innuendo in the suggestion, then the couple laughed.

'I'd like that.' His voice had picked up a deeper undertone and Scarlet smiled to herself.

She'd never actually seen her mother in action before and it was illuminating and even amusing. Until she heard her next suggestion.

'Bring your son. Scarlet is housebound at the moment and would welcome some company from the hospital.'

Scarlet lifted her head in shock and whacked the back of it against the doorframe. 'Damn!' She rubbed her head and tried to catch her mother's eye. Cameron started to cry and Scarlet sighed. She'd kill her mother. She wished she'd never left the house.

'I can't believe you did this.' Scarlet was viciously chopping celery, still fuming thirty minutes before the visitors were due.

Vivienne was her usual serene self. 'It will be fine. If you hate it that much, take yourself off to bed. But I was hoping you'd change out of your jeans into a dress. Make an effort to brighten yourself up.'

The doorbell rang. 'Oops, they're early.' Vivienne glanced at her reflection in the microwave door and tidied her hair.

Scarlet glared. 'I'll get it and I'm not changing.'

Her mother just laughed. 'It's good to see a bit of fight in you, dear. All this moping around was starting to worry me.'

When the door opened Sinclair thought Scarlet looked sombre but fabulous in tight black jeans and a ribbed sweater.

Her 'Please come in' belied the fire in her eyes and

he wondered if he should turn around and come back another time. Then his father pushed past, smiled blithely at Scarlet and sailed into the house. That was it, then.

He cleared his throat. 'Pleased to see me, I gather.' Sinclair watched her grit her teeth and the funny side of the situation caught up with him. She was no more impressed when he smiled.

'My mother's idea and it *is* her house.' She gestured him in with her hand. 'Please come in.'

He looked around with interest. It was a welcoming house with lots of plants and interesting knick-knacks. The last time he'd been here he hadn't noticed anything but Scarlet. 'Well, that deflates any pretensions I may have had.'

'I'm sure you have enough to go around.' The sound of a baby's cry floated down the stairs.

She shot a look at his face and then away. 'Excuse me. I have to attend to *my* baby.' She spun on her heel and left him.

Sinclair stared after her. Had she stressed the 'my' in 'my baby'? Her jeans clung lovingly as she took the stairs two at a time and he was sure they said, Come hither.

It had been hell staying away from her the last two weeks and he didn't fight the impulse to follow her now.

Sinclair tracked the soft croon of her voice and when he found the room he leant on the doorpost of the baby's nursery. The walls were pale blue but he was more interested in the big white wooden rocking chair facing the window.

The black sweater she'd been wearing lay in a heap on the floor and the light shone off the paleness of her slender shoulders as she sat in the chair. The white lace of her bra strap bisected the soft curve of her breast as she bent over the baby in her arms, reminding Sinclair of a Renaissance painting.

He swallowed the lump in his throat. How could he have walked past her all that time? It was still difficult to fathom how he'd never thought to look beneath the mask of the meek midwife to the true Scarlet inside.

Maybe she hadn't heard him come up the stairs, and for a fleeting second he wondered if he should creep away.

But he couldn't. The empty hollow in his heart formed by that one night with Scarlet began to ache as if the raw edges had just been exposed again. She was married, damn it. He should never have come.

Sinclair watched her rest back into the chair and sigh as her hair fell across her face and breast. The sight of her clenched his gut with desire and he knew he had it bad. For a man who spent most of his days around breastfeeding or labouring women, the sight of Scarlet and her baby blew him away like no one ever had.

Scarlet must have sensed his presence because when she turned her head she didn't look surprised.

He felt like a peeping Tom. 'I'm sorry,' he said, 'but you both looked so beautiful I couldn't leave.' The simplicity of the statement embarrassed him but it obviously upset her. A tear rolled down her cheek and he cursed himself for an insensitive monster. 'I'll go.' He turned to leave.

'It's all right, Sinclair.' She sniffed. 'Perhaps you could pass me one of those tissues. I seem to have

the labile emotions of the post-partum period off pat.'
She pointed to the dresser top.

He moved into the room and passed them to her.
She looked so alone with her baby. He wanted to
gather them both up in his arms—which should have
surprised him, but didn't. Even the realisation that he
wished Cameron were his own son didn't surprise
him. 'Why isn't your husband here for you?'

She remembered her mother's advice. 'We're going
through a rough patch. Let's leave it at that.'

His eyes narrowed with concentration at the first
positive news he'd had. 'How far can I leave it?'

'A lot further than you are at the moment.' He
sensed her mood change and almost sighed as she
glared at him. Back off, he warned himself.

He held up his hands. 'Sorry.' He crouched down
beside her chair and some herbal scent drifted from
her hair. It reminded him of the night he'd buried his
face in the fragrance of it and had felt silken strands
slither across his chest. The band around his heart
tightened.

He couldn't prevent himself from moving closer to
breathe in her scent and she turned her face towards
him. Her soft lips were so close and his hunger
gnawed at his control like a trapped rat. But that's
what he would be if he took advantage of her vul-
nerability.

Instead he sat back on his heels. He still had to ask
and his voice was husky when he spoke. 'Can you
tell me why I never saw you again after that night?'

Scarlet closed her eyes and he thought she wasn't
going to answer him.

She didn't look at him when she spoke. 'What can
I say? It was a turning point in my life and out of

character for me. Afterwards, I needed some time to find myself again.'

The answer was disappointing but he couldn't leave it alone. 'You can't deny it was special. Can you?'

She turned towards him and her eyes narrowed. 'If you want me to say that, I will. But it's in the past, so let it drop, Sinclair.'

Her attitude confused and, he had to admit, infuriated him. His eyes hardened. 'What if I don't want to drop it?'

Scarlet glared. 'Then leave and don't come back.' They glared at each other and neither of them softened. Finally she tossed her head in disgust.

'Perhaps you could inform my mother I'll be twenty minutes or so on your way out.'

That had been dumb. He had no right to harass her because of one incredible night. He needed to think this through and he couldn't sit across the room from her tonight and stay sane. He stood up. 'If that's what you want,' he said, and after one last glance at the baby in her arms he left. He heard her blow her nose as he walked down the stairs. All he'd achieved had been to upset her and most likely stop himself from sleeping for the next few nights. He should stay away from her.

Scarlet dried her eyes. Damn the man. How was she going to cope with him when she went back to work? She could ask him to leave her mother's house but she wouldn't be able to evict him from the ward. Maybe working at Southside wasn't such a good idea.

CHAPTER THREE

FOUR weeks later on her first day back at work, Scarlet couldn't calm the butterflies in her stomach. She dreaded her first contact with Sinclair.

To settle back into being inconspicuous was harder than she'd imagined.

Irritated by the length of her hair, Scarlet had decided to cut it to a short bob. She didn't realise that her shoulders were straight and her chin pointed up instead of down as she walked in with her bag.

'Welcome back, Letty.' Michelle stepped up and hugged her, and Scarlet hugged her back. 'Love the hair.'

Scarlet put her hand up to her neck and smiled. She had missed the camaraderie that flourished in the unit.

'Thanks.' She grinned at her friend. 'Do you think you could call me Scarlet? I'm used to that now. And I kept Robin as my work name.'

'No problem. And when do we get to meet Gerry the geologist? Still in some out-of-this-world place?'

'I'm afraid so. It's not working out. Marriage may not have been the brightest thing I've ever done.' Scarlet could hear herself rambling again and she looked away. 'I don't want to talk about it.'

Michelle hugged her again. 'No worries. How is your gorgeous son?'

'Gorgeous.' Scarlet's eyes softened. 'He's six weeks old now and takes the expressed breast milk from the bottle really well as long as I'm not the one trying to give it to him.'

'Well, it's going to be busy today, so yell when you need your lactation break. We don't want you to explode.'

Scarlet laughed. 'At least you guys understand. So what's on the agenda for the day?'

'Two kids in the crib in oxygen, one first-time mum in the birthing unit whose waters broke yesterday evening but she's taking a while to establish labour and a oxytocin induction of labour is booked for this afternoon.'

Scarlet was itching to get into it. 'Can I take the birthing unit?'

Michelle grinned as she agreed to work in the nursery for the shift. 'But you won't get it all the time.'

'I suppose it's a bit different from when I used to say, "whatever you want",' Scarlet acknowledged wryly. 'I've changed in the last few months working away.'

'What was it like, not having medical back-up, when you lived in the valley community?' It was obvious Michelle was fascinated by the idea.

Scarlet smiled at the memories. 'Sometimes it was scary, but it was an incredible experience, being present for the births there. Before I went, I knew I was midwifery-trained but now I have so much more confidence. Confidence that when women are left to their own devices, they'll progress in their own time. When they listen to their own bodies they are capable of directing their own labours, as opposed to being patients who have their labours managed for them. I'm afraid I've become an advocate to let the mother do it herself.'

Michelle's eyes danced. 'Well, good luck. This should be a hoot. Sinclair McPherson is coming in to start a drip to speed labour for the woman in unit two—in half an hour.'

'Sinclair McPherson, eh?' Scarlet supposed it was too late to ask to work in the nursery now without making an issue out of avoiding Sinclair. She squared her shoulders. 'In that case, I'd better go help her find some contractions—then he won't need to interfere. Catch you later, Michelle.'

Scarlet scanned the written notes as she walked down the corridor. She could handle this. She had to. When she opened the door to the birthing unit Scarlet smiled warmly at the young couple. They looked very nervous as they waited for the doctor to arrive—with mother-to-be on the bed and her husband holding her hand as he sat beside her on a chair. Scarlet shelved her own nerves. This was a prime example of people lacking confidence by not being in their own environment.

'Hi, Jill. Hi, Peter. I'm Scarlet and I'm your midwife today.' She walked over and shook both their hands before perching on the edge of the bed.

'Before the doctor comes, I'd like to have a chat about the type of birth experience you were hoping for. It really helps if you can fill me in on what you expect today will bring.'

They both looked at her as if she'd just spoken Russian until finally Peter took one chewed fingernail out of his mouth and grinned. 'We expect a baby. The ultrasound people told us it's probably a boy— and they said he was about eight pounds.'

Scarlet's eyebrows lifted. 'Crikey. They didn't leave much to the imagination, did they? Don't be

surprised if some of that's different. It's pretty hard
to judge until a baby is naked and on the scales.'

She smiled encouragingly at Jill. 'He left the labour
part to your imagination. What are you imagining today, Jill?'

The two women looked at each other and Scarlet
saw the apprehension behind the younger woman's
smile.

'We went to antenatal classes so we have an idea
now how it works,' Jill said. 'But I guess—more pain
than I have now.' Jill pleated the sheet. 'Heaps more.
And my mum said it would probably be hard—and
I'd get stitches because the baby's eight pounds and
I'm so small.'

Scarlet glanced at Peter's face as he paled. She noticed him squeeze Jill's hand. Good. He'd be a worthy
support for his wife. She'd love to get her hands on
Jill's mother with a few suggestions about induction
of fear before labour.

'OK. How about I give you some good news?' She
smiled at them both. 'Your body is designed to give
birth naturally, and your baby is designed to fit
through whatever size pelvis his or her mother has.
So we need a little faith here. Yes, there are excep-
tions to the rule and that's why you're in a hospital
and not out in the desert, doing it by yourself. But
that's for your doctor to worry about—not you. We
have to give them some job while you carry on and
do it yourself. So believe you can do it— I do!'

They both nodded, Jill almost relaxing.

'OK. The next thing is to actually allow your body
to set or establish itself into labour. There are a few
things you can do to encourage that. Most impor-
tantly, you have to trust it. If you're lying down, all

tense, waiting for pain, do you think your body is going to think this is a safe place to let out all your hormones? It's a hard place to begin labour.'

Jill nodded. 'So what do you think I should do?'

'I'm not being smart here—' Scarlet's voice was gentle '—but what is your body telling you to do?'

Jill looked at her husband. 'Well, it is difficult to lie still when the pains do come. Maybe I should get up and walk around?'

Scarlet smiled. 'Let's do it, then.' She hooked a small footstool over to the bed with her toe.

Jill bit her lip. 'But aren't I supposed to wait here for the doctor? The night nurse said that he was coming to put in a drip and make my contractions come more quickly.'

Scarlet glanced at her watch. They still had twenty minutes. She was pushing it. 'If you have faith in your body and relax, maybe your body will move into labour by itself. Then you wouldn't need any synthetic hormones to start what your body can do for itself.' Time was against them and she had to temper it. 'Or less of them if you do still need a drip.'

Jill scrambled to the edge of the bed. 'I like the sound of that—I hate needles.'

'Me, too.' Peter stood to help his wife off the bed. 'I faint at the sight of blood.'

They all laughed and Jill started to waddle around the room. The look of surprise on her face when the next pain came more quickly made them all laugh again.

'I think I should have been doing this all morning,' Jill said as she slowly rocked her hips during the contraction. 'It's much less painful when I stand up than when I lie down.'

'Remember that for later in labour.' Scarlet turned to Peter. 'If you notice her complain about the pain then it's time for her to think about doing a different activity.'

She looked at Jill. 'The shower is terrific as a change from walking. But stay off the bed for long periods. Think lots of positive thoughts and trust your body. OK?'

They both nodded.

'I'll slip out and get you some ice and water. Fluids are important, too.' She waved as she left the room.

Scarlet crouched down to get ice from the ice machine and she could feel her nerves tighten. Sinclair would be here soon.

She hadn't seen him since the night he left early from her mother's. Old Dr McPherson had continued to call on her mother at least once a week—at least that relationship seemed to be sailing along smoothly—but he hadn't mentioned his son to Scarlet.

She scooped another paddle of ice into the jug and nearly tipped it all out as she tilted her watch to check the time again. She grimaced. Today would be the worst—it would get easier over time. She hoped.

'Sister Connors?' The deep voice came from behind her left shoulder and she dropped the jug at her feet. Ice skidded across the polished floor in all directions and she didn't even notice the cold on her own legs. She stared at the splashes of water across Sinclair's shoes and up his trousers—then she looked at his face.

He wasn't a happy camper. 'Damn,' he said as he brushed the water off the material with the back of his hand.

His annoyance stiffened her spine and she stood up. 'Damn yourself—you scared the living daylights out of me. And it's Sister Robin at work.'

To her surprise, his eyes creased with a brief flash of amusement. 'My apologies, Sister.' He was at least eight inches taller than she was and his good posture used it all.

'What did you do to your hair?' He raised his hand halfway to her face before he seemed to realise what he was doing and it fell away.

Typical man. Why did men rave about long hair? She frowned. 'Had it cut.'

With the brevity of her answer he blinked and his face became his usual professional mask. 'When you've finished with the ice, perhaps you could escort me to see my patient.'

Scarlet winced at the word. At that moment a domestic assistant bustled up to Scarlet with a mop. 'Don't you worry, dear. I'll sort this out if you want to go with the doctor.'

Scarlet sent her a grateful smile. 'Thanks.' She quickly scooped up some fresh ice from the machine and dashed after Sinclair. She caught up with him down the corridor and had to skip a couple of times to match his stride. That didn't improve her mood.

Scarlet glared at Sinclair. 'You know, I've never mentioned it before but when you call a healthy pregnant woman a "patient", I find it offensive.'

His eyes widened and she looked away and then back again. What the heck was she doing? The actual concept was true but to blurt it out at this inauspicious moment was bizarre.

Sinclair blinked, gave her a strange look, looked around as if for inspiration of what had caused that little outburst and then ignored her. He continued down the corridor towards the birthing unit.

Scarlet gritted her teeth. He was going to overlook her comment. How big of him. And she'd just decided to pull her head in, too. If he was going to ignore her then she might as well go the whole way.

'I'd like you to consider withholding Jill's intravenous Syntocinon until lunchtime to give her body a chance to do the job itself.'

That made him stop. 'Do we have a problem here?' He looked her up and down. There was no amusement now and a long moment of silence fell as they glared at each other. There was a brief softening in his eyes and for a moment she thought he might be willing to discuss it.

Then his face hardened again and he finally spoke. 'What happened? Did you wake up this morning and decide to be an obstetrician?'

Not likely. She stared levelly back. 'What a ghastly thought.' Scarlet winced in exaggerated horror. 'No. I'm much more useful as a midwife! I thought I might advocate more strongly for my client's wishes. If that's all right with you, Doctor?' The words tumbled out unbidden and afterwards she decided she must have had a devil in her.

In the past, she'd tried to steer the doctors unobtrusively towards a less dogmatic approach to birth, often with little success. While the desire to help each woman find the most rewarding birth had always been there, now it consumed her and she guessed she'd have to pay the price with a less peaceful existence. More pushing, less steering. Oh, brother, life was going to be interesting if she couldn't control herself.

Sinclair just looked at her. 'Ah. But is this your

client's wishes or yours, Sister? I gather your time among the valley dwellers has altered your hospital values.' She had his full attention now and he actually snorted.

'Nevertheless, I've found that the suggestion of hastening the first stage of labour does seem attractive to *most* women. But let's find out, shall we?'

Sinclair knocked on the door and then stood back for Scarlet to precede him into the room. He didn't leave her much room. She wasn't sure if he'd done it on purpose, but she was determined she wouldn't brush against him as she slid between him and the door. It was a tight fit.

Jill was smiling at something Peter had said and Sinclair raised his eyebrows at Scarlet as if to say he couldn't see labour starting on its own.

'Good morning, Peter, Jill.' Sinclair shook Peter's hand.

'Good morning, Doctor,' the couple chorused, and Scarlet had to resist the urge to roll her eyes.

Scarlet really hadn't taken any notice of the ritual of doctors' visits but this one was getting right up her nose. Jill was the most important person in this room, not the fellow in the suit. Or was that just *her* attitude this morning?

Sinclair must have remembered that because he turned towards Jill. 'How are you, Jill? Night Sister said you've been bothered by contractions for the last few nights and your waters broke last evening?'

Jill nodded as she unobtrusively settled herself on the bed and clasped her hands over her stomach.

'And now Day Sister Robin thinks you might progress on your own if we give you more time before we start a drip. How do you feel about that?' To give

Sinclair his due, he didn't try and influence Jill either way when he spoke to her.

'I'd like to try, if you don't mind the wasted visit this morning.'

Sinclair's smile was noncommittal. 'I'll just have a feel of your tummy if you don't mind. I like to see which way your baby is pointed on the way out.' He smiled and Jill eased down in the bed, eager to please.

Scarlet lifted two pillows out from behind Jill's head to help her lie flat and she heard Sinclair rub his hands together to warm them. The sound drew her eyes to those long-fingered hands she remembered so well. They were almost elegant as they gently palpated the mounds and hollows of Jill's stomach to draw a mental picture of the baby's lie.

A warm knot formed low in her belly and Scarlet grudgingly conceded his technique was excellent—and not only in palpation of pregnant abdomens. She frowned at the wayward thought and shifted her feet to distract other areas of her body from responding.

'I'll come back at lunchtime and we'll see how you're going.' His voice brought Scarlet back to the present and she rubbed the sudden rush of goose-bumps on her arms to make them disappear before he noticed them. Thank goodness goose-bumps didn't come out on your face for everyone to notice, she thought grimly.

Snap out of it, woman, Scarlet admonished herself. She followed Sinclair but paused to smile reassuringly at Jill. 'I'll be back in a minute.'

'Thanks, Doctor.' Peter was out of his chair to accompany them to the door and to close it after them.

Sinclair stopped a few paces up the corridor and held Jill's chart out to Scarlet.

'Happy?'

Just that one word and the inflection he used sent her blood pressure soaring. She bit back a very un-Letty-type expression and contented herself with a less inflammatory comment.

'Yes, thank you, Doctor.' She took the chart without touching him. 'We'll see you at lunchtime, then.'

It was as if he could read her mind. The side of his mouth quirked but that was the only sign she could see to make her think he found the conversation amusing. He turned and left her staring after him until he walked out the front door.

Sinclair whistled as he went down the steps two at a time. Well, that had taken her by surprise. It looked like Scarlet was having problems getting the mouse back in the cage. He grinned.

He was pretty sure things weren't going smoothly with the husband, who still hadn't showed. He was beginning to wonder if there really was a Mr Connors. And she hadn't changed her maiden name at work.

His brow furrowed. He wondered how much chance there was that it was true. If there was no husband then who was Cameron's father? Maybe he and the baby should get better acquainted.

When Vivienne opened her front door, she had the little man he'd come to see in her arms. Perfect.

'Hello, Sinclair. To what do we owe the pleasure of this visit?' Scarlet's mother stepped back and gestured him in.

'I had a few minutes before I'm expected back at my rooms and wanted to thank you. Your company has really cheered my father's state of mind.' He watched Cameron's bright eyes follow the voices from face to face and he couldn't help the grin that softened his face.

'That's very sweet of you. Come through to the lounge. I'm just giving Cameron his bottle.'

He walked after her and sank back into the lounge, trying to relax. He searched his mind for something to say. 'So he's on formula now that Scarlet is back at work?'

Vivienne shook her head. 'No. Scarlet wouldn't have that. He's on expressed breast milk and takes it well.' She looked up at him with a smile. 'If you'd like to finish giving him this feed I'll make us a cup of coffee, if you have time.'

'No problem. I don't get to do this part much.' He reached up and took the baby from her arms, along with a bib and the warmed bottle.

Vivienne was strangely quiet for a moment but then seemed to rouse herself. 'Black and no sugar, like your father?'

Sinclair was staring down at the infant in his arms. He looked up and replayed the question in his mind. 'That's right, thanks.'

As he watched her leave the room he could feel the weight and heat of the baby in his arms. It felt good. He looked back at Cameron making little slurping noises as he greedily sucked on the teat. As if aware of Sinclair's interest, the baby stopped for a moment and gazed solemnly back at the big person above him before his face broke into a huge gummy smile that dribbled milk around the edges.

'You're a cheeky boy, aren't you?' Sinclair heard the soppiness in his voice and shook his head. What was he doing? But the kid was a real cutie. He jiggled the teat in the baby's mouth and Cameron looked away and started sucking again.

'Here you are.' Vivienne carried a teatray into the room. She placed it carefully out of Cameron's accidental reach on a small table beside Sinclair's leg, and he could smell the fresh scones from three feet away. His mouth watered.

'You'll end up with me as a permanent visitor if you spoil me like this,' he said.

'You're welcome any time. As is your father.'

Which reminded him. 'I've been concerned about Dad for a while. He doesn't seem to have the get-up-and-go he used to have. Though he's much brighter since he started coming over here.'

'We're all getting older and our needs change,' she said as she poured his coffee and even jam-and-creamed his scone for him. 'I think he needs a new interest.'

Sinclair frowned. 'I think he should retire. I know he'd like to see me settled and he's mentioned grandkids a few times.'

'That's natural.' Vivienne smiled at her own grandson.

'I've even started thinking the same thing myself. Lately.' He looked down at the tiny bit of milk left in the bottle and took the teat from Cameron's mouth. 'He finished that quick!'

'Give him to me, and I'll wind him. Have your coffee.'

Sinclair found himself strangely reluctant to give up his charge but handed him to his grandmother. He had to get back to work soon anyway. 'Thanks. I enjoyed the experience.' Cameron's gaze stayed on Sinclair's face as he was handed over. His little head swivelled for one last look before his grandmother tucked him up over her shoulder to bring up his wind. Sinclair picked up a scone and gazed thoughtfully into his coffee. Five minutes later he left.

Back on the ward, Scarlet frowned as she dropped into the ward nursery to update Michelle.

'How'd you go with Dr McPherson?' Michelle flashed her a look as she juggled the syringe she held connected to the tube into the baby's stomach and the bottle of warmed milk that kept the syringe from emptying.

'We've got until lunchtime to see if Jill establishes labour on her own.'

Michelle wiped off a droplet of milk that had fallen on the roof of the incubator. 'Well, that's a win. You know that anyone draining amniotic fluid is usually sped on their way if they haven't started labour by daylight.'

Scarlet grimaced. 'Yes, but when you think about it, why?'

Michelle frowned at the syringe barrel. 'Because the safety bag's broken. Risk of ascending infection. You know that. What's your point?'

'My point is—what's the rush? As long as basic hygiene is maintained, the risk of infection is much smaller than the risk of interference from a synthetic induction of labour. She could even go home to wait for labour to begin if she knew how to watch for signs of infection.'

Michelle disconnected the syringe and capped the end of the tubing. The tiny baby that lay in the incubator was still asleep. She straightened the kink in her back and turned to look at her friend. 'So you'd like to teach her to use a thermometer and take her own temperature at home until she goes into labour?'

Scarlet nodded emphatically. 'A mother should know how to take a temperature anyway, and she could at least have a little longer to let nature take its course.'

'That's fairly radical, mate. They'll be screaming about germs in the outside world.'

'Right. So there's no germs in a hospital?'

Michelle laughed. 'I'm not against you. And I'll admit you do see a run of interventions like epidurals once they start with inductions. It's just a new idea, that's all.'

Scarlet was emphatic. 'And after epidural can come the inability to push as efficiently, leading to maternal exhaustion and forceps which moves us on to episiotomy.'

Michelle bit her lip to stop a laugh escaping. 'The poor woman. You're full of doom and gloom. I hate to think how radical you'll be by the end of your first week.'

Even Scarlet had to laugh at that. 'Sorry. Softly, softly, used to be my motto. I think I've been possessed by a demon.'

Michelle put her hand on her shoulder. 'Nah. You've always thought like that, you just didn't say much before. It's amazing how having your own baby stiffens your spine for the women you care for.'

'Thanks, Michelle. I'd better go and see how Jill's contractions are coming on.'

Michelle waved her away with a grin. 'Go get 'em. Can't wait for the lunchtime episode when Dr McPherson comes back.'

*　*　*

By one o'clock, Jill's contractions were more regular but not as close together as Scarlet would have liked. Jill was pacing the room and resting during the contractions by leaning over pillows stacked on a bedside table.

Peter was coaching Jill to sigh before and after each pain. Scarlet listened to the baby's heartbeat with a handheld Doppler every half-hour and she'd been careful not to unintentionally apply pressure on Jill to perform a miracle.

Jill sighed after a particularly strong contraction. 'Do you think he'll still want to start the drip?'

Scarlet hoped not. They could progress from where they were now, although it could take a few more hours. 'I really couldn't say, Jill. If he does, it will shorten your labour but sometimes the pains can be stronger than you would normally expect so quickly.'

'My mum had all her babies induced. But, then, she had epidurals as well.'

'People weren't as ambulant years ago. They had to endure most of their labours on the bed. Let's cross the epidural bridge if we come to it.'

There was a knock at the door and Sinclair walked into the room.

He didn't look at Scarlet and she couldn't tell by his voice what he was planning. 'So how's it going, Jill?'

'I think it's coming along.' Unlike the doctor, she didn't have a problem looking at the midwife for confirmation.

Scarlet supported her. 'Five-minutely regular contractions, lasting forty-five seconds and moderately strong. Foetal hearts are fine at 140 beats per minute.'

Sinclair turned to face her. 'Have you a foetal heart monitor printout for me?'

'No, but I could do a quick trace for you now if you need one. When Jill lies down the contractions go off a bit and we wanted to establish labour.'

The paper readout he'd requested showed the baby's heart rate and heart rate reaction to the contraction of the uterus. It was also proof of the regularity and length of contractions. Scarlet wanted to say monitors caused intervention but thought she might have used up Sinclair's tolerance for the day. It had been a calculated risk that he wouldn't ask for a foetal heart trace as she'd wanted to keep Jill off the bed as much as possible.

Sinclair narrowed his eyes for a moment then turned to Jill. 'What would you like, Jill? I can start the drip and you'll probably have your baby by teatime or you can continue on your own which could possibly take up to the early hours of the morning.' He smiled. 'Of course, there's always the chance you'll be quicker than any of us expect. Perhaps you'd like to discuss it with your husband.'

Scarlet's mouth almost fell open. She had to admit, Sinclair had done a turn-around and she admired his ability to be flexible.

He gestured for Scarlet to move to the side of the room to give the couple some privacy. He looked at Scarlet sardonically and his voice only carried to her. 'I'm on call tonight so I can still be here for the baby's birth. Of course you, Sister Robin, will be off duty.'

The smart comment slipped out. 'You could always pick me up on the way through if it made you feel any better.'

He surprised her again when he grinned.

'I'm sure we'll manage.' He looked back towards the bed and saw that the couple was ready to tell him their decision.

'Well?' Sinclair smiled to imply it didn't worry him either way.

Peter squeezed his wife's hand. 'Jill would like to let nature take its course, if that's OK with you, Doctor?'

There wasn't a flicker of surprise on Sinclair's face. 'Not a problem. I'll drop in to see you both after work and, of course, the midwife on duty at the time…' he shot an ironic glance at Scarlet '…will call me if you need me.'

Somehow Sinclair drew Scarlet out the door with him. When she shut the door behind them, he stopped and turned and she almost ran into him. There was nowhere to go. As she tried to step around him, she realised again how broad his chest was. But he didn't touch her.

'So the gloves are off, are they?'

She could detect the faint trace of his aftershave and it brought back memories that seemed to surface when she least wanted them. She moistened her lips with her tongue until she noticed him staring at her mouth with an arrested expression on his face. Her heart thumped and her tongue hid.

'I'm not sure what you mean, Dr McPherson.' Scarlet's voice almost squeaked and she cleared her throat. Drat the man. He was invading her space *and* her brain.

'With your new-found zeal for natural birth it looks like the chance of you fading back into obscurity is really not an option. Is it, Scarlet?'

'If you mean I'll defend the mother's right to have as natural a birth as possible then I suppose I'll be noticed. Yes.'

She heard him mutter, 'It should be interesting.' And with one more sardonic smile, he left. The guy was winning the exit-line stakes and it was starting to annoy her.

After lunch, Jill's labour suddenly took off and Scarlet, Jill and Peter spent the last of Scarlet's shift in the shower.

'I've never spent two hours in a bathroom with two women before,' Peter commented as he rubbed soap on Jill's lower back during a pain.

Jill was holding the hand-shower directed on her bikini line. 'And you never will again,' she said, and sprayed his shirt. Then she closed her eyes and moaned gently with the force of the next contraction.

Scarlet murmured encouragement when Jill needed it during the height of the contractions. She also tried to keep her soaked nursing shoes from under the erratically aimed water stream.

Jill's eyes widened and her breathing changed. Scarlet looked up and smiled at Peter.

'It's getting close now. I'll go and give Dr McPherson a ring.'

She nudged the delivery trolley closer to the bathroom door and dialled Sinclair's number.

'Dr McPherson.'

'Hello, it's Scarlet in Maternity. Jill's in second stage.'

'That was quick. Isn't she clever?' She could hear the smile in his voice. 'I'll see you soon,' he said, and hung up.

CHAPTER FOUR

ONCE committed to birth, Jill's baby boy decided to be born in a hurry. Sinclair arrived in time to see the delivery of the placenta on the shower chair in the bathroom. The horrified expression on his face was a picture Scarlet would treasure.

'We do have perfectly good labour ward beds. Patients are upright just like a chair—only they're designed for this.' He gestured towards Jill and her baby then he shrugged. 'I'm obviously not needed here at this late stage. Congratulations, Jill and Peter.' He inclined his head towards Scarlet. 'Sister Robin.' Then he returned to his rooms without saying anything else to her.

Scarlet had to admit she was disappointed she hadn't had the chance to rub it in a little, but the new parents were over the moon with the course Jill's labour had followed.

'Thanks, Scarlet.' Peter kissed her in his exuberance.

'He's gorgeous. You were both wonderful.' For Scarlet, Jill's obvious pride in her accomplishment was all the thanks she needed. And Sinclair's interference had been avoided. She felt like pumping the air with her fist.

At changeover report late that afternoon, Michelle introduced Scarlet as the new 'bathroom' midwife of the unit. The only fly in the ointment was Tessa, who sat with a disapproving look on her face through the recital of the excitement.

'People come into hospital because they know we'll deliver their babies in a safe place. Would you call the bathroom safe?' Tessa raised elegant eyebrows.

Michelle frowned and Scarlet looked at Tessa with a calm smile. 'Women don't need to be flat on their backs to give birth in a protected environment. They assume more control for the birth if they're in an upright position.'

Tessa shrugged. 'That's right, you're the one who advocates home births.' She glanced around at the other midwives. 'That's even more unsafe.' She tossed her hair. 'I don't understand how any midwife could agree with such a risky undertaking.'

This was one duel she wouldn't lose. Still serene, Scarlet replied. 'I don't suppose you would.'

Michelle raised her eyebrows and stifled a grin. She stood up. 'Well, that's report finished. I have to go. Come on, Scarlet.'

Scarlet spoke to the frowning Tessa. 'I know you've been back around a year now, but you haven't had the chance to see the side of midwifery that exists on the home-birth front. It's wonderful and exciting. Treat those people with respect and they'll treat you with respect.'

'I don't need respect from them.' Tessa looked Scarlet up and down. 'Or you.'

For the first time the barb slid off harmlessly. Scarlet shrugged. 'That's attractive.' And she walked away to follow Michelle.

When they were outside, Michelle touched Scarlet's arm. 'Sinclair was taking her out before you came back. But I don't think things are running as smoothly as they were. She blames you, I'd say.'

'We've always been at odds.' Scarlet stopped as Michelle's incredible words sank in. 'Why would she think I have any influence over Sinclair?'

Michelle shrugged innocently. 'Maybe it has nothing to do with it.'

Scarlet brushed that reasoning away. 'I think Tessa looks down on home-birth clients, home-birth midwives and, at a guess, me in general. For a change, it doesn't worry me. I just hope that if any of the women from the valley come in with complications, Tessa isn't on duty.'

By the time Scarlet arrived home that afternoon she was glad to sit down to feed her baby.

Later, when she rested on the settee with a sated Cameron over her shoulder, her mouth twitched. There had been some moments of unusual interest today, not the least being those involving Sinclair.

Cameron stirred and Scarlet patted his back.

'Did you miss me? Your mummy had a good day. I missed you.' She kissed his tiny fingers. 'Were you a good boy for your nana?'

Cameron burped and Vivienne caught the conversation as she carried in a tray with fresh tea and scones. 'He was fine. So all went well, then?'

'It's great to be back, and we had a lovely birth today.' She propped Cameron up on two pillows beside her on the settee.

'I'm glad. So how many shifts have you been rostered for?' Vivienne poured the tea and set it down in easy reach of Scarlet.

'Thanks, Mum.' She took a sip and sighed as the

cinnamon and apple flavour hit her mouth. 'They want me to do six shifts a fortnight. Is that too much childminding for you?'

Vivienne reached across and tickled Cameron's foot.

'No. As long as it's not too much for you. I enjoyed looking after him. He can come with me if I want to go somewhere when you're working.' She lifted her own cup. 'Did you see Sinclair today?'

'Yes.' She compressed her lips and left it at that. Then she caught her mother's look and smiled. 'OK, it was a bit awkward in the beginning, but I got so busy I didn't have time to worry about him.'

'Did he mention he dropped in to see me this morning?'

Scarlet's cup clattered on the saucer and some of the tea splashed over the edge. Suddenly she felt sick. 'He what? Why? Did he ask to see Cameron?'

Her mother continued to serenely sip her tea. 'Calm down, you're overreacting. He was on his way back to his rooms and dropped in to have a few words about his father.'

'I don't believe it. He suspects something.' She shot a look at her mother. 'You didn't say anything to make him suspicious, did you?'

Vivienne lifted her head and raised an eyebrow. 'I'll pretend you didn't say that, Scarlet. If you think I have a problem with my loyalties then I'm surprised you're happy to leave your son with me.'

Scarlet rubbed her brow with her free hand. What was she thinking? 'I'm sorry, Mum. You're right. I had no right to say that. My only defence is that man makes me crazy. I don't want him to have rights over my baby.'

'I think you'll come to realise that he *does* have rights over the baby who belongs to *both* of you, but it's up to you to come to that decision, not me. Now, drink your tea and I'll tell you about his visit.'

Scarlet's hand shook slightly but she obediently picked up the cup and took a sip. That was one decision she'd never come to. Cameron didn't need a trapped father in the background and Scarlet needed to remain in control.

Vivienne went on. 'Sinclair's father has been depressed and unwell lately and Sinclair wanted me to know that he felt Frank's visits here seem to be helping his state of mind.' She glanced across at her grandson. 'Sinclair didn't ask to see Cameron, perhaps because he didn't have to. I was giving him his bottle when Sinclair arrived.'

'Did he look at him?'

Vivienne frowned. 'Will you listen to yourself? The man is an obstetrician. He loves babies! Of course he looked at him. He took over the feed while I made some coffee.'

Scarlet shook her head. She wasn't sure what upset her the most—the fact that she was frightened Sinclair might decide Cameron could be his baby or that he had nursed her baby and she hadn't been here to oversee it. 'Well, Sinclair should get married and have children of his own.'

Vivienne sighed and gave her one of those I-do-not-understand-you looks. 'Perhaps you should picture him with another woman and think about how it would make you feel. It may just happen. Sinclair seems to think if he settles down his father may retire and start to take it easy.'

'Good. If Sinclair married that would be the best thing. Then I could get on with my life the way I want to.'

Vivienne snorted. 'That sounds fascinating. Why should Sinclair's marital status affect the way you get on with your life?' Scarlet didn't answer. Vivienne put down her cup. 'I think I'll go out. I have a letter I want to post. If you think of an answer to that question I'd be interested to hear it.'

Scarlet watched her mother leave the room. Cameron was asleep and she should put him to bed before he woke again. She sighed and picked her son up carefully to walk with him balanced over her shoulder. She didn't want to think about her mother's words but they followed her up the stairs.

Would Sinclair suddenly decide to marry? He'd been perfectly happy as a bachelor all these years. And whom would he marry? She remembered Michelle's words. Tessa?

How ironic if she was frantically worried about trying to keep him from finding out about his son when his present plans didn't include a baby by another woman anyway.

But the voice inside whispered that it would be easier for her to plan for her future with the temptation gone if he was married to someone else. She flinched. Yeah—like cutting off your leg so you didn't get an ingrown toenail.

No. Sinclair was his own problem. Gerry the geologist was here to stay as her baby's father and she wasn't going to be Sinclair's last fling before he settled down and married some perfect doctor's wife.

*   *   *

Just before tea, the doorbell rang, and Scarlet had a premonition. When she answered it, she found she was right. Her eyes narrowed.

'My mother's not here, Dr McPherson.' After a quick glance at Sinclair's face she concentrated on the top button of his shirt but had to fight against the urge to linger at the gap in his unbuttoned collar. There was something incredibly attractive about a strong man's neck.

'I've asked you before to call me Sinclair.' He stepped closer. 'I haven't come to see your mother. May I come in?'

Scarlet drew a breath and stepped back out of his way. 'Mum said you'd already dropped in this morning.' Scarlet caught a curious look from the neighbour across the road as the woman stared at the doctor visiting twice in one day. 'For goodness' sake, come in before the whole town wants to know why you're here.'

He brushed past her and she was sure it was deliberate as the heat from his body went right through her.

His voice was casual. 'You'll really have to practise your door greetings, Scarlet. Your welcome lacks a certain warmth.'

She was warm all right. Damn him. She willed herself to relax as she walked in front of him into the lounge room. Scarlet gestured for him to take the armchair and when he had she perched on the settee furthest away from him. 'And your visit is inappropriate—I'm a married woman.'

'Are you?' The words were almost inaudible. He settled himself into a lounge chair and crossed his long legs.

At least one of them was relaxed, she thought bitterly, and then his words sank in. Her heart thumped and she shot a look at him. 'What did you say?'

He looked back at her innocently. 'Your husband. Yes, I want to ask you about him, but before I do...' He brushed that subject away and smiled his killer smile at her. 'Congratulations on the birth today. In fact, my clients were very clever and think you're wonderful. Note I didn't call them patients.'

Scarlet's guard slipped a little as she remembered her own pleasure at Jill's baby's birth. Her voice was earnest. 'I'd wanted to talk to you about suggesting that women go home again when they're in early labour. Even those with broken waters like Jill. We would explain about risk factors and safety issues. Give them a chance before speeding up their labours artificially.'

Sinclair's gaze was sceptical. 'Maybe early labours we could think about, but ruptured membranes need more discussion. Write me a protocol—I promise I'll read it and we'll see.'

It was better than nothing. She didn't know whether to go on or not. 'Drugs aren't always necessary. Women are very powerful when they set their minds to it.'

He gave a half-strangled laugh and sat forward in the chair. 'They're powerful all right. It was an interesting morning.' She could tell he wanted to change the subject.

Scarlet was trying to keep track of all nuances but his humour kept her off balance.

'So your mother told you I visited. Did she mention I spent some time with Cameron?'

Scarlet's heart started to thump again and the nau-

sea was back. 'In passing, she did.' She swallowed a
lump in her throat. 'So?'

Sinclair stared back at her blandly. 'He's a fine boy.
Don't you think he's handsome? Like me?' His question dropped onto her without warning and she
jumped off the settee as if scalded.

She dared a glance at him. 'Cameron?' Her mind
went blank and she couldn't think what to say.
'Cameron has nothing to do with you.' She looked
away, straightened her shoulders then forced herself
to meet his eyes. 'He looks just like his father.' She
had her voice under control but the rest of her was
like jelly. She needed a minute to think. 'I'm sorry.
Would you like a cup of tea or coffee?'

He looked at her consideringly and to her relieved
surprise he accepted the diversion and nodded his
head. 'Yes, please. Coffee, black, no sugar.'

A trivial thought crossed her mind. She'd slept with
the man and didn't know how he took his coffee.
Snap out of it, she told herself. At this moment she
felt as if she'd played into his hands but she couldn't
think how. 'I won't be a moment, then.' She turned
towards the kitchen but before she'd gone three paces
he was walking beside her. She could feel the heat
from his body again against the skin on her outer arms
and shoulders. And everywhere else in her body.

His voice came from beside her ear. 'Let's have it
in the kitchen, shall we? It's much friendlier in there.'

Alarm bells were ringing and she couldn't think
how to get rid of him. Where was her mother? Scarlet
fell back on the only defence she had. 'I don't think
my husband would want me to become too friendly
with you, Sinclair.' She stressed the 'husband'.

'Ah, yes. The geologist you've been going through

a rough patch with. I've been meaning to ask about him. When is this elusive traveller coming home?' He moved to the small kitchen table and sat down.

Thankful for a little more space from him, Scarlet tried to settle her nerves. She kept her back to him as she filled the jug and plugged it in because she could still feel him watching her every movement. 'Probably some time in the next month.' She stared blindly out the kitchen window.

Sinclair's voice made her blink. 'Tell me about him. He must have swept you off your feet.'

Scarlet forced herself to leave the safety of the sink and approach the table. 'Yes, he did.' She laid out the cups. 'Coffee, you said?'

He nodded, undiverted. 'Let's see. Your birthday was in November and Cameron was born in August...'

He was playing with her as well as the dates, and suddenly Scarlet refused to let him have it all his own way. She cut him off. 'Look, Sinclair. If you want to get sordid here, let's do it! I met, fell in love with and slept with Gerry a fortnight after I slept with you. You used contraception, he didn't. End of story. Now, if you don't desperately need this coffee, I'm not enjoying this conversation and would appreciate it if you left.'

'So you're saying there's no way that Cameron could be my son.'

She wasn't ready for this. 'Good Lord, did you think that?' She crossed her fingers behind her back and prayed she wouldn't get hit by lightning. Then she looked him straight in the eye and said in what she hoped was a firm, convincing tone of voice, 'Cameron is not your son.' She switched the jug off and took his cup away. 'You have no right to come here and make these accusations. Please, leave.'

Sinclair rose and looked down at her as she stood rigidly in front of him. Her beautiful hair was shining like a cap and she had a hunted look in her eyes. Had he put that look there? Sinclair sighed. Wishing Cameron were his son wouldn't make it true. And now she'd categorically stated he wasn't the father he'd better accept that. But he was still having trouble doing so.

'Yes, I'll go. I'm sorry if I've upset you.' He hid the depth of his disappointment behind his bland smile. 'I won't bother you at home again. But I'll watch for the next instalment of alternative birthing at Southside.' He stood up but had time for one more parting shot. 'Perhaps you could try and have a birth on the bed for a change.'

The next day at work began calmly. Scarlet was on shift with Tessa and the air between them was chilly. The good news as far as Scarlet was concerned was that Tessa preferred the orderliness of the nursery and the doctors' rounds with the postnatal women. Scarlet preferred the emotions of the labour ward.

There were only two women in labour. Apparently Sinclair had been in and had offered one the option of going home for a few hours until the contractions were stronger. Scarlet couldn't keep the grin off her face when she heard that.

So there was no problem with the delegation of the work. As long as Tessa stayed out of her way, Scarlet was happy. She was about to move down the hallway to meet her clients when the phone rang.

'Maternity, Scarlet speaking. Can I help you?'

'This is Nina Wade. I'm an independent midwife.' The name rang a bell. Scarlet had heard good reports of Nina during her time in the valley. The woman's voice was brittle with tension and Scarlet felt her own nerves tighten. 'I'm bringing a client of mine—Karen Wilson—in for a probable emergency Caesarean section for ante-partum haemorrhage and foetal distress.'

'How long before you get here, Nina?' Scarlet began to weigh up what she could achieve to streamline the admission before they arrived.

'Fifteen minutes, if not quicker. We're about to leave.'

Scarlet frowned. 'What about the ambulance?'

'There isn't time. She started bleeding heavily ten minutes ago and I haven't been able to locate the baby's heartbeat since the bleeding started. I think it could be a marginal placenta praevia. Karen didn't want any scans during pregnancy, so I can't be sure.'

Placenta praevia was when all or part of the placenta was across the cervix in front of the baby's head. If the cervix dilated, as it had to in labour, the edges of the placenta would start to separate from the womb and open blood vessels would be exposed.

Scarlet winced. Without the empty uterus needed to clamp down on itself and control bleeding after placental separation, both mother and baby were in serious trouble. Caesarean section was the only way out for baby or mother. 'OK. I'll see you as soon as you get here. Is there a doctor that your client has seen at all?'

'No. She refuses to see a male doctor because of a past history I'll fill you in on when we come in.'

'Right.' Scarlet glanced at the big hospital clock on the wall. Seven-ten a.m. Theatre staff wouldn't be in for another fifteen minutes. 'I'll start the wheels turning. Good luck.'

'Thanks. You never know what reception your client's going to get when you bring her in for a complicated home birth.'

Scarlet nodded to herself and tried to send positive thoughts down the phone line. 'We're here for you both. See you soon.'

'Thanks, Scarlet.' But the foreboding in Nina's voice was easy to hear.

Scarlet pressed for a new line and punched in Sinclair's direct office line. She'd been worried how she would face him after his visit yesterday but now she would be glad to see him as soon as possible.

'Dr McPherson.' Sinclair's voice was calm as usual and Scarlet drew a breath to match his own even speech.

'It's Scarlet here. I've an unbooked, complicated home-birth admission with query placenta praevia. She's bleeding quite heavily and no foetal hearts have been heard since the bleeding started ten minutes ago. She should be here in ten to fifteen minutes.'

'Contact Theatre. I'm on my way. Has she had any previous ultrasounds?'

'No. The midwife said the client hadn't wanted a scan.'

Scarlet heard him sigh. 'Right,' he said, and hung up.

Scarlet punched in the nursing supervisor's number and repeated the information. The supervisor would contact the theatre staff and arrange for another midwife to cover the birthing unit while Scarlet was in Theatre with the new admission.

The phone settled into its cradle and Scarlet looked

up to see Tessa. She'd caught the gist of the conversation and was glaring at her.

Tessa curled her lip. 'The parents should be ashamed of themselves for risking their baby by having a home birth in the first place.'

Scarlet winced and shook her head. 'You know, Tessa, your attitude sucks.' Scarlet would have laughed at the expression on Tessa's face if there hadn't been an emergency coming in. She'd relive it later. 'It's people like you whom home-birth parents are afraid of meeting if their instincts tell them to come here for help.'

Tessa shrugged. 'That's just tough. If they want us to fix their mistakes, they'll have to wear it. If I was the doctor expected to save the day, I wouldn't be happy either.'

Scarlet struggled to contain her anger. 'You're wrong. Choosing home birth isn't a mistake—it's merely a choice. Those parents deserve our unbiased support because they haven't taken that decision lightly. I don't have the time to discuss it with you now, but after this is over I'll make the time.' Scarlet met the other woman's eyes. 'And if you allow these people to feel your displeasure I'll make sure the nurse manager and every other person who works here knows that your professional attitude is severely lacking.'

Tessa drew herself up to her full height. 'Are you threatening me?'

'If you like,' Scarlet threw over her shoulder as she hurried down to the spare birthing unit to set up for the admission. 'Are you going to help or not?'

'I still don't know how you could consider risking

a child's life by encouraging home births,' Tessa said as she grudgingly followed her down.

'When any woman in labour rings here in trouble, it's just the same as if they'd had an emergency in the birthing unit. I can't see how any self-respecting midwife or doctor could withhold the support and comfort a woman and her family need.' Scarlet flipped down the hinged cover that disguised the oxygen outlets and hung a mask over the nozzle before moving over to the bed.

'I'm not encouraging home birth, I'm respecting parental choices and providing support in a medical emergency to people who need it. Now, truce till later.'

Scarlet was only giving Tessa a small portion of her thoughts as she stripped off the bed and organised intravenous fluids to be ready for insertion as soon as the mother arrived. Depending on the size of the haemorrhage, the mother could be in hypovolaemic shock by the time she got there, which would further decrease any placental function that was left for the baby.

Tessa assembled the notes, gown and trolley for immediate transport to Theatre, and both midwives looked up when the doorbell rang to signal the arrival of the newcomers. They sprinted up the hallway.

'I'll get the resuscitation trolley ready for baby. That I believe in. You can look after *them*,' Tessa said, and peeled off to the nursery.

Good, thought Scarlet as she grabbed a wheelchair and hurried to the door to help the pale woman, supported by her husband and the midwife.

'Hello, Karen. I'm Scarlet. Sit in the chair here and we'll get you to bed.' As soon as the woman had half collapsed into the chair, Scarlet wheeled it around and pushed her swiftly down the corridor back to the birthing unit. 'Doctor is on his way and will confirm what we can do for you as soon as he gets here.' She sent a brief reassuring smile towards the woman's frantic husband. 'We do have a theatre on standby.'

The next five minutes were hectic as Nina changed Karen out of her clothes into a gown and took Karen's blood pressure while Scarlet inserted an intravenous line into the free arm. The oxygen mask blew cool oxygen into Karen's face as she lay back with her eyes closed.

'Her blood pressure is stable at 90 on 50 but her pulse rate is still 130. The bleeding seems to have slowed a little on the way in,' Nina said, 'but I still can't hear baby's heartbeat.'

Scarlet looked up from where she was taping the cannula in place. She turned the fluid rate up to maximum and gestured with her head towards the large foetal heart-rate monitor. 'Try ours. It's pretty powerful—you might have more luck with the larger transducer.'

'Thanks.' Nina handed over an antenatal card. 'Here's the information I have for your records.'

Scarlet took it and reached behind the bed for the notes Tessa had assembled to be filled out. Nina gently slid the ultrasound cap over Karen's stomach to try and pinpoint baby's heartbeat.

Tessa came in with Sinclair at the same time as a very faint clop-clop of a slow foetal heartbeat finally emitted from the cardiotocograph machine.

Everybody sighed with relief because at least now they had a hope to cling to that the baby would be all right, though the heart rate was half of what it should have been.

'I'm Dr McPherson.' Sinclair stepped up to the bed and met Scarlet's eyes for a moment as he lifted Karen's wrist. He grimaced at the maternal pulse, which was galloping along at twice the baby's speed.

'This is Karen and George Wilson,' Scarlet said, 'and their midwife, Nina Wade. Karen's baby is due in two weeks by dates and has had no previous problems during the pregnancy except for this sudden painless bleeding which started after her first contraction today.'

Sinclair nodded and shook George's hand. Karen looked up briefly, and the fear in her eyes when she saw the male doctor must have alerted him. He was very gentle and explained everything he was going to do. His examination of Karen was brief but thorough and afterwards his voice was decisive.

'Right, Karen and George. Your baby needs to be born by Caesarean section as soon as possible. I imagine your midwife mentioned the possibility?' He looked at Nina, who nodded. 'We'll need to use a general anaesthetic as there isn't time for an epidural to work for baby to be born with you awake. That also means George can't come in either.' He looked at them to make sure they understood. George nodded and Sinclair continued, 'Have you eaten anything in the last four hours?'

Karen didn't answer or meet his eyes, but George spoke up.

'She didn't feel like breakfast and all she's had is half a cup of water about an hour ago.'

Sinclair nodded. He briefly ran through the risks of a Caesarean and anaesthetic and the immediate postoperative period while Scarlet completed the paper-work.

Karen signed the consent and the theatre wardsman arrived with the trolley to transport them across to the theatres.

'Let's go, then. I'll brief the anaesthetist and see you over there.'

'Is it all right with you if Nina comes in with me, just to observe?' Scarlet wasn't hopeful of his response but again he surprised her when he looked at the other midwife and smiled.

'Karen might feel less anxious among strangers and I'm sure Nina would like to see this birth through. I don't have a problem if that's what Karen wants.'

This time Karen did meet his eyes, although it was only a frightened glance from under her lashes. Sinclair acknowledged her mumbled thanks with a nod and left to prepare the theatre for their imminent arrival. Scarlet spared a second to stare after him thoughtfully. The man had potential.

The convoy of patient trolley, midwives and George, whom they would leave outside the plastic theatre doors, was rolling along the corridors.

Nina touched Scarlet's arm and mouthed a 'thank you' for including her in the theatre group. They both knew how much of a relief it would be for Karen to know that her own midwife would be there, too.

George leant over and kissed his wife's cheek as they entered the theatre complex. 'I'll be right here,' he said, and his voice shook. He gazed longingly after them as the trolley pushed through the swinging doors.

CHAPTER FIVE

SCARLET squeezed Karen's hand. 'Nina and I are going to get changed into special clothes and this sister here will ask you the same questions that I asked you over at Maternity. By the time she's finished with you we'll almost be ready. We'll see you inside. OK?'

Karen's eyes were filled with tears as she nodded her head. Scarlet smiled down at her. 'We won't be gone long.' She met Nina's eyes. 'We'd better move fast.'

Within minutes they were pushing open the operating-theatre door, garbed in hats, masks and gowns like everyone else.

The midwives were just in time to help the staff move Karen across to the operating table. Karen's limbs quivered with fright and her eyes stared, wide with fear, but she settled a little when she recognised Nina's familiar face behind her mask.

'Not long now, Karen. Hang in there,' Scarlet said quietly. 'Think welcoming thoughts for your baby for when you wake up.'

The anaesthetic took effect and Scarlet and Nina stepped back out of the way. Scarlet checked the resuscitation trolley equipment after its trip over from Maternity. The overhead lights and heater were on and the oxygen and sucker were ready to use as soon as baby was born.

'I'll get scrubbed to take the baby when Doctor gets him or her out,' Scarlet told Nina, and hurried into the scrub room. When she returned in sterile gloves, Sinclair hadn't wasted any time. It was only a few minutes until the baby's arrival.

Scarlet winced at the pea-soup green meconium-stained amniotic fluid that gushed out of the now exposed uterine cavity, and tightened her grip on the sucker. Meconium, or the first blackish-green stool passed by the newborn, was sometimes released inside the uterus. This was usually because of post-maturity—a pregnancy that extended past the time the baby should have been born—or sometimes because of the infant's stress in the womb. A baby became stressed when the usual placental function of oxygen supply was impaired by a medical condition or haemorrhage. Karen's baby had probably been stressed and passed the meconium stool when the placenta had started to separate from the uterus and the oxygen supply had decreased.

As a birth attendant, Scarlet's job was to prevent the meconium that floated in the amniotic sac from sticking to the baby's lungs when it took its first breath.

'Here it comes.' Sinclair's voice drifted quietly across to Scarlet and she angled her sucker into the baby's mouth as the head appeared at the surgical opening of the uterus. Thick meconium covered the baby's face and the scrub sister quickly wiped it away with a sponge. The sound of the sucker was the only noise in the theatre.

As the rest of the baby—a boy—was born, Sinclair quickly clamped and cut the cord so that Scarlet could carry the newborn over to the resuscitaire. The child was limp and pale as Scarlet laid him on his back and the anaesthetist left his unconscious patient with his anaesthetic nurse to intubate Karen's son. A thick glob of meconium slithered up the sucker tubing as he viewed the baby's throat and vocal cords with the laryngoscope to check for further meconium.

'Good thing he didn't take a breath before now, with that sitting there,' the anaesthetist commented, and Scarlet silently agreed.

But *now* would be nice, she silently urged the baby.

The anaesthetist slid a breathing tube into the baby's throat and after only a few puffs on the air bag on the other end the baby started to twitch and grimace. Suddenly the baby coughed and a weak cry could be heard over the sound of the sucker and oxygen flow.

Scarlet looked up and caught Nina's expression as the other midwife sagged against the wall. Nina had squeezed her eyes closed but tears trickled down her cheeks as she realised the baby was alive.

Unfortunately, baby wasn't out of the woods yet, Scarlet thought grimly as they removed the tube and placed the oxygen mask over his nose and mouth. His breathing was rapid and shallow and his little ribs receded with every breath.

'Let's get him over to the nursery crib and into some decent oxygen as quickly as we can,' the anaesthetist murmured, and Scarlet nodded.

Scarlet looked back towards Sinclair. 'His respiration rate is over eighty. I'd like to transfer him into the crib.'

Sinclair's forehead was creased. 'Do that. I've rung the paediatrician at the base hospital and he should arrive by the time you get baby settled. I'll come over as soon as we finish up here.'

*   *   *

The next hour passed in a blur. Scarlet had to admit that Tessa was an experienced neonatal nurse and used to handling very sick babies. She took over the care of Karen's baby but was less than welcoming to Nina and George. Scarlet drew the father and midwife away for a much-needed cup of tea as soon as the baby was settled.

'He looks a little better already, don't you think?' Scarlet said as she removed the teabag from Nina's cup.

'His colour's better but I wish I knew how his lungs are.'

'The X-rays will be back soon,' Scarlet said.

Nina took the cup gratefully and sipped at the hot fluid. 'Thanks, I needed this.'

'If he's fine, it will be because you and George brought Karen in so quickly. You did a great job. Have a break and I'll let you know as soon as Karen is back from Recovery.' Scarlet squeezed George's shoulder. 'I have a new admission in labour so I'll catch you later.'

As she walked down towards the birthing unit, Sinclair stepped out of the nursery.

'Sister Robin? The X-rays are back.'

Scarlet tried to pick up the prognosis from his voice but he was going to tell her anyway. 'The paediatrician doesn't think we need to transfer baby to the base hospital if he stays stable. Where's the father?'

'That's wonderful.' Scarlet gestured with her head. 'They're both in the tearoom.' Sinclair nodded but before he could turn away Scarlet reached out and put her hand on his arm. 'Sinclair?' The warmth of his body seeped into hers. Unconsciously she tightened her grip on him without realising what she was doing.

He tilted his head. 'Scarlet?' The amusement was back on his face.

She grimaced. 'Be nice. Don't be hard on them because they wanted a home birth.'

He looked at her thoughtfully. 'You must be thinking of someone else. I'm always nice.' He squeezed the hand on his arm. 'Don't worry,' he said, and walked away.

Her hand dropped and she stared after him. She was beginning to realise how many preconceived ideas she'd had about him. And not all of them had been right.

By the time Scarlet made it home that afternoon, she was mentally exhausted. They'd had another quick birth by a first-time mum and Scarlet had been the birth attendant. Again Sinclair hadn't made it on time but at least they'd been standing beside the bed when the baby had been born. She smiled tiredly. Sinclair hadn't said much except that she was getting closer to the bed.

When Scarlet came in for her next shift, she sighed when she saw Tessa.

The ward was busy and neither midwife said anything as they sat down to hear the night sister's report. Without discussing it, Scarlet went off to the birthing unit and Tessa took the nursery. When she had a moment, Scarlet promised herself a long talk with Karen.

Carrie and Jim were having their third baby in three years and Scarlet had met them with their previous children. They'd arrived just after midnight and both looked exhausted this morning, even before the baby was born. It had been a long, hard night.

Scarlet smiled sympathetically at the grey smudges under their eyes. 'Hi, guys. It's lovely to see you again.'

'Hi, Letty.' Jim peered at her badge. 'How come it says Scarlet?'

She laughed. 'I used to shorten my name but I'm going the full Monty now. So that's my name.'

She sat on the edge of the bed and smiled at Carrie. 'I've had my own baby since I last saw you, so now I'm sure you must be Superman and Superwoman to cope with your two daughters, let alone another one almost here.' She took Carrie's wrist and felt her pulse. 'So, how are you doing, Carrie?'

The huge grey smudges under her eyes were even larger than her husband's. She could barely raise enough energy to speak. 'I'm tired and I'm sick of it. Everything aches and I don't think I can handle many more of these contractions.' Two tears slid down her cheeks along the faint line where others had been. 'How long do you reckon it's going to be?'

'Night Sister said Dr McPherson's been in. She said he suggested an epidural and that you were five centimetres.' Scarlet picked up the hand-sized book with circles to illustrate the dilatation of the cervix. She pointed to the one that was five centimetres wide.

'Five centimetres is excellent. The slow half of labour is finished with and we get to the exciting half now. Can you hang in for a little longer?'

Carrie sighed. 'I'm terrified to have an epidural but I've felt so uptight this pregnancy, and now this labour has been so slow. The idea of it all happening without me knowing about it is becoming attractive. I don't think I can do it any more.'

Scarlet frowned and stroked the woman's leg in

sympathy. 'Can I just do some observations and then we'll have a think about your options and how you can get more comfortable?'

'OK. But I'm cold and I'm not getting up and walking around later. I know what you're like, Letty-Scarlet.' The weak grin that accompanied the comment drew one from Scarlet in response.

'I'll get my thinking cap on.' She busied herself and took Carrie's blood pressure, which was slightly elevated, and her temperature, which was down.

Baby's heart rate was steady on 140 and unaffected except by a nice increase in rate at the start of the next contraction. Scarlet kept her hand on Carrie's tightening abdomen, timing the contraction from start to finish. Carrie gave a shuddering sigh at the end of it.

Scarlet lifted her hand and wrote down the timing. 'That was a big one. OK. How does this sound? If I run you a big warm lavender bath, you could just lie in the water and rock with the contractions and you wouldn't have to walk around. The heat all around you will ease the pain and it should make you feel a bit sleepy, which isn't a bad way to spend the next hour or so. It won't take all the pain away but will help.' She spread her hands. 'I throw myself on the mercy of the court.'

Carrie smiled. 'That sounds pretty good, actually. But I thought if I lay in the bath too soon it could slow my contractions.'

'Your contractions are strong and regular, so it should be fine. Actually, half-dilated or more is the best time to hit the water.'

'OK. I'll try it.'

The next hour Scarlet spent sitting on the side of

the bath with Jim as they reassured Carrie that she was doing brilliantly. The pains were coming long and fast and Scarlet could tell when the stormy time of transition hit Carrie. Transition was that time at the end of first stage and before the start of the pushing contractions.

Carrie sat up in the bath and her eyes widened. 'I want to go home.' She looked at her husband. 'Now!'

Scarlet caught Jim's glance and smiled. 'What does that sound like to you, Jim? You've seen Carrie go through this twice before.'

'Transition?' His eyes were hopeful and he looked at his wife with love and sympathy in his eyes. 'Hang in there, honey. You're nearly home.'

She met his eyes and nodded. 'You'd better be right—or you're dead,' Carrie muttered as she sank back in the water.

By the end of the next contraction Carrie's breathing had changed and Scarlet could tell she'd moved on to second stage. It would only be a couple of pushes before the baby was born.

'OK, Carrie,' Scarlet reached for the towel. 'Time to get out and have this baby.'

Carrie didn't open her eyes and Scarlet could tell she was pushing. She couldn't help her own excitement. She'd always wanted the option of water birth at Southside but there was no policy for them in the hospital and that meant it wasn't on. 'Hello, Carrie? We have to get out of the bath, friend. We're not allowed to have water babies here.'

'Sorry. Can't do it,' she gasped. 'I'm not moving.'

Scarlet rubbed her neck. 'OK…' She stood up and reached for the cordless phone and dialled Sinclair's number. He wasn't going to be happy about this.

'Dr McPherson.'

'Sinclair?' Scarlet didn't even realise she'd called him by his first name. 'It's Scarlet.' She didn't pause for him to answer because this baby wasn't going to wait. 'Carrie Wright has just started second stage and she's in the bath.'

'Well, you got her in there—get her out!' Scarlet winced at the bark.

She tried to make her voice soothing. 'I have tried.'

'Try harder. You know it's not on. Don't do this. I'm on my way.' Scarlet lifted the phone away from her ear as he slammed his receiver down.

She looked across at Jim who was trying to coax his wife out of the bath. Carrie wasn't having any of it.

Scarlet couldn't help a tiny grin at the thought of Sinclair driving grimly up the road towards them. But she might find herself out of her job if she didn't think of something fast.

Carrie was pushing steadily now and Scarlet knew that most of the time third babies knew their way out quicker than their siblings had. 'Right, then, Carrie. That's fine. As long as you're comfortable. If you won't leave the water then the water is going to have to leave you. Sorry about that. There's no policy to say we can't have the baby in the bath without water, though.' She grinned and reached in to pull the plug out of the bath to let the water drain away.

'Grab me a couple of warmed towels so she won't get cold, please, Jim, and press the buzzer for the other midwife to come in.'

Scarlet had a fair idea what Tessa was going to think of this development but the other midwife was the least of her worries. The water was taking for ever to disappear and she could see a small crescent of baby's head between his mother's legs.

She couldn't figure out why the water wasn't lower then she noticed that a facecloth was stuck in the plughole. Scarlet reached in and plucked it out but couldn't help thinking that the situation was turning into a farce.

Tessa arrived on the scene, took one horrified look at the baby's scalp showing under the water and had a fit. 'Get this woman out of the bath.'

Jim jumped. Scarlet glared and said, 'Thank you, Sister.' She used the first thing that came into her mind to prevent a scene at what should be a wonderful event. 'Dr McPherson is aware of the situation.' She gestured to the bath. 'The water is draining now, as you can see. Perhaps you could manoeuvre the delivery trolley in here so we'll have something to cut the cord with.'

Tessa opened and shut her mouth before turning away to get the trolley.

The water was below the level of the baby's head now, and Scarlet settled back down on the side of the bath. 'Pop the towels over Carrie, Jim. We don't want her to get cold. OK, Carrie, nice and gentle now.' Scarlet cradled the baby's head in her hand as the last of it eased out of the birth canal. She slipped her finger in beside the baby's neck to feel for the cord then drew back again.

'No cord. Gentle push when you get the next pain, Carrie.'

The outer door opened and closed and Sinclair appeared at the bathroom door. There was no room for him to come in with the trolley barring the door. His eyes met Scarlet's over the top of everyone else and promised retribution later. But his voice was calm. 'Well done, Carrie.'

Scarlet looked back at the baby and watched the tiny head swivel forty-five degrees to restitute the shoulders under the pubic bone.

First the anterior and then the posterior shoulder slipped out and she lifted the rest of the slippery baby up onto his mother's abdomen, where he slid around a bit until his mother held him. The thick umbilical cord trailed after him.

Jim's voice carried over the baby's cry. 'It's a boy. We've got our boy.' He leant over, kissed his wife and son and wiped the tears from his face.

'Congratulations,' Sinclair said dryly. 'Perhaps you should call him Neptune.'

Scarlet kept her head down to hide her smile as she waited for third stage to be complete. Once the shiny placenta was accounted for, she checked Carrie for any grazes and pronounced herself done. She straightened her shoulders and glanced up at the door.

Sinclair indicated with his head that he wanted to see her outside, and she nodded resignedly. He spoke to Jim. 'I'll just borrow Scarlet for a minute. Enjoy your family in private for a few moments.'

Tessa shot her an I-hope-he-gives-you-hell look and sashayed back to the nursery.

Scarlet sighed and looked back at the family in and around the bath then slowly removed her gloves and gown. Carrie was proud of herself because she hadn't needed an epidural and that made it worth everything.

She closed the birthing-unit door behind her and leant against it. Sinclair was standing, tapping his foot in the corridor.

She lifted her head and met Sinclair's eyes. 'Yes, Doctor?'

He stared at her for a moment and the silence lengthened uncomfortably. Scarlet refused to blink and for a moment she thought it was going to turn into a children's staring contest. Her eyes were starting to water and a bubble of laughter was tickling at the bottom of her rib cage. Nervous laughter. He might make her crazy but she knew she was alive when he was around.

Then he spoke. 'Congratulations, Sister Robin. Two bathroom deliveries in your first week. Perhaps you'd like to have a baby over the sink next?' He tilted his head in query.

Scarlet narrowed her eyes. 'The object of the game is for the mother to be confident and comfortable wherever she wants to be, Doctor.'

'No. The object of the game, Sister Robin, is to maintain sense and safety for all concerned. And that rules out water birth. If you'd left that water in I would have seen you out of your job. You do realise that?' He glared at her.

Her shrug was infinitesimal but he saw it. His lips thinned. Scarlet felt a small thrill of satisfaction at penetrating his control, but hastened into speech before he blasted her. 'That was a consideration in the removal of the plug. But mostly I did it because I'm inexperienced at water birth and it wasn't safe practice to learn at that moment.'

He seemed to have regained control. 'Well, then, we can be thankful for small mercies.' But the sarcasm was thick in his voice.

Scarlet wasn't finished. 'But I am planning on becoming accredited in water birth.'

He narrowed his eyes. 'Not in my hospital.'

'Perhaps it's time Southside and you moved into the twenty-first century, Doctor.'

'We don't need you to push us. Like you're pushing your luck at the moment.' He stared at her for a moment then shook his head and his voice changed. 'What are you doing?'

She could feel the depth of his look, as if he were trying to see inside her. For a minute it threw her and he took advantage of her shock.

'Are you trying to make me notice you?'

That made her head fly up: 'You amaze me. Dream on, Dr McPherson. If I was trying to make you notice me, you wouldn't have to ask. You'd notice. I'm here for my clients and no other reason. I'm sorry if you don't agree with my philosophies and I will try not to contravene any hospital protocols.' She took a deep breath, astounded her response had come out coherently. It might be time to beat a strategic retreat, though. 'If you've finished, perhaps I could return to my client.'

He gave a short harsh laugh and Scarlet winced. 'By all means, Sister, carry on. But, please, remember that they are my "clients", too.' He spun on his heel and presented her with his back.

Scarlet could feel the adrenaline pumping around her body as he walked away. A sudden film of tears pricked her eyes and she dashed them away. Like hell she'd cry over words from that man. She turned back to the birthing room and leant her forehead on the door for a moment before going in. She took three calming breaths and plastered a smile on her face before turning the handle.

Sinclair passed the sister's desk without even noticing it.

'Excuse me? Sinclair.'

Tessa's voice intruded on his thoughts. He dragged his mind away from the image of Scarlet standing up to him in the corridor. 'Yes, Tessa?'

'I'd just like you to know that I didn't realise Mrs Wright was in second stage while still in the bath. I was just as horrified as you were.'

Sinclair's brow furrowed in distaste. That was strange. A minute ago he'd been furious, but he wasn't sure he liked to hear someone else condemn Scarlet's midwifery. 'Thank you, Sister. And I thought all you midwives here stuck together. Good evening.'

He watched her sink back into the chair and realise that it hadn't gone as planned. He even felt sorry for her. But he wasn't in the mood to do anything about it. He had enough trouble trying to stay one step ahead of another certain midwife.

As he walked down the steps towards his car he suddenly smiled. At least Scarlet had pulled the plug out. The last few days had been anything but boring.

She amazed him with her newfound zeal for natural labour and delivery. He didn't have any real objections as long as the patients were happy and he didn't consider it dangerous. And preferably if it didn't involve him crawling around on the wet bathroom floor to deliver a baby. As long as all these alternative birth positions didn't get out of hand. He certainly couldn't call Scarlet a mouse now!

She had looked so beautiful when she'd been spitting fire at him that he'd wanted to kiss away her anger and turn her passions to a more desirable avenue—but she was married to some absent idiot and adultery was a sin.

But there was Cameron. Regardless of whether Scarlet's husband was in the picture or not, Sinclair felt a special affinity with the child.

After spending that short time alone with Cameron the other day, he'd needed Scarlet to categorically confirm that Cameron wasn't his son. She'd done that. He just wished he could accept it!

The next week passed quietly by Scarlet's standards. Dr Roe was on call for the two evening shifts Scarlet worked, and except for his morning rounds, Sinclair wasn't seen by the maternity staff at all.

One client was booked for a Caesarean section and, except for suggesting the family bring their own music choices into the operating theatre, Scarlet kept a low profile with the medical officers.

The cold war between Scarlet and Tessa reached new heights when Tessa continued to recount Sinclair's fury at Scarlet's attempted water birth.

After the morning staff, including Tessa, had gone home, Michelle took Scarlet aside to hear the full story.

'So did he rip through you like Tessa says?'

'No. The woman's a witch. He just mentioned that if I hadn't pulled the plug he would have taken it further.' Scarlet's eyes brightened. 'But it was so close. We nearly had our first waterbaby.'

Michelle grinned. 'Maybe we'd better get someone up from Sydney to give us an in-service on it in case accidents happen.'

'I said I'd go away and get accredited—but imagine if we held our own seminar here. I'm sure Sinclair would love that.'

'Sinclair, eh?' Her friend looked her up and down. 'So what's the story between you and Sinclair McPherson?'

Scarlet shrugged. 'Nothing.'

'Yeah, right.' Michelle tilted her head. 'On his side, when you disappeared, he sure was interested in where you went.'

Scarlet shot a look at her friend. 'What makes you say that?'

Michelle rolled her eyes. 'He asked if we'd heard from you every couple of days until we started to ask why he was so interested. Then he shut up. When I mentioned your phone call about you and Gerry getting married, he started the third degree again until people began to notice.'

Michelle watched her expression. 'Tessa's telling people they're secretly engaged but haven't announced it yet. I'm not sure if I believe her but I'd hate to see you get hurt again.'

Scarlet met her friend's eyes. 'I'm immune to Tessa at the moment. I'd say I was doubly immune to men. Though I've had a nasty reaction to the immunisation process.' She tried out her new decision on her friend. 'My marriage is over. Gerry isn't coming back.' She desperately wanted to say there never had been a marriage—she hated the way one lie turned into many. Was her mother right? Should she have brazened it out? But then she'd have to tell Michelle who the father of her child was. Not a good idea when the father himself didn't know.

Michelle compressed her lips sympathetically. 'I'm sorry, Scarlet. I'm rabbiting on and men are probably the last thing you want to talk about.'

'I'm fine, really, Michelle. Actually I'm sort of relieved. Just not into men at the moment.' They both looked up as the front door opened.

A handsome young man in cut-off jeans waved at Scarlet. He placed a large brown-paper-covered parcel on the floor.

'Speak of the men-devils.' She glanced over her shoulder at Michelle with a smile as she walked towards the door. 'Come and meet Keir. He's from the community and is the daddy of one of our little success stories up there.

'Hi, Keir. This is my friend Michelle. What are you doing here?'

He leant across and kissed Scarlet on the cheek. 'I've brought you a thank-you present.'

Scarlet looked down at the large parcel and felt the tears prick her eyes. Presents in the community were made and not bought so receiving them was doubly special. 'You didn't have to do that, Keir.'

'Of course I didn't but this is something I think you'll really love.' He crouched down and stroked the parcel and a big grin stretched across his face. 'I made it myself. It's waterproof. Open it.'

Scarlet bent down and untied the woven ribbon. Suddenly, the paper fell off to reveal a curved wooden stool. It was thickly lacquered and looked almost like an open fronted toilet seat.

Scarlet laughed in delight. 'It's a birthing stool. How fabulous.' She looked up at Michelle and her eyes sparkled. She looked back at Keir. 'I can't wait to use it. Thank you, Keir. That's the best present I've ever had.'

They both stood up and she threw her arms around Keir just as Sinclair walked in the door.

CHAPTER SIX

SINCLAIR had been watching Scarlet's animated face through the glass in the door as he approached Maternity. He couldn't see whoever it was she'd crouched down to talk to but just watching her made him smile. Until he opened the door and had a perfect view of her launch herself at some man beside her.

When he saw her kiss the man he felt the sickness in his stomach like a sudden bout of food poisoning. He grunted, glared at them both and stepped past them to the desk. To complete the picture he nearly tripped over what looked like a wooden garden seat in the middle of the corridor.

'What is happening to this place?' he almost snarled at Michelle as she appeared at his shoulder. She looked startled.

He sighed and held up his hand. 'Sorry, Sister. Bad day. I've dropped in to see my antenatal patient, Mrs Jones, so let's do it.' He picked up her chart and shot Scarlet a disapproving look as he stalked past with Michelle on his heels.

He didn't know what he was going to say to Mrs Jones, but he'd think of something. He'd really come to see Scarlet. Another bad idea in a long line of bad ideas. Sinclair ground his teeth. He had to find out who the guy was.

He looked down at Michelle. 'I suppose it is about time the husband came back.'

Michelle shook her head. 'Scarlet said he's not coming back.'

Sinclair shot a look at her from under his brows but she didn't elaborate. 'Then who's he?'

'Keir's from the valley community. He brought Scarlet a present.'

Another man in her life. He frowned when he heard the laugh in Michelle's voice. Now, what did she think was so amusing? 'I gather the present is that thing I nearly fell over?'

He had the feeling there was something going on here and he'd get to the bottom of it soon. But all she said was, 'Yep.'

They walked into the two-bed ward, and he focussed himself enough to make general enquiries, but the whole time, peripherally, he was aware of Michelle's statement that Scarlet's husband wouldn't be coming back. He concentrated again on Mrs Jones and made sure he didn't rush the visit. They agreed on a suitable discharge date and said goodbye.

Michelle shrugged as she walked ahead and he could tell she thought he was acting strangely. He knew that he was. He'd been unstable since November the previous year.

When they came around the corner of the ward, the corridor in front of the entrance door was empty.

Now where were they? he thought grimly. Probably in some room, kissing.

Scarlet appeared from the unit manager's office. She looked so vibrant and happy he couldn't tear his eyes off her.

No one else was with her and she grinned cheekily at him. The sickness cleared from his gut like magic.

'Dr McPherson. I've something I want to show you.'

He thought he heard Michelle mumble something as she walked away but he didn't ask her what she'd said. Sinclair moved towards Scarlet, drawn by invisible strings. When he entered the office and the door shut behind him with a click, he realised he'd pulled it closed as he'd come through.

The mood in the room swung from Scarlet's exuberance to mutual awareness of their cramped isolation from the rest of the ward.

Her tongue passed nervously over her lips and his eyes were drawn to the sheen of moisture left behind on the erotic pink roundness. Unable to help himself, he reached out and stroked the dampness on her bottom lip gently. It was incredibly soft.

She flinched and her eyes widened.

His hand snapped back to his side and he shook his head. What the hell was he doing? 'I'm sorry.'

At least she looked as pole-axed as he felt. He jammed his libido back in its box and tried to remember why he'd shut himself in a room with Scarlet if he wasn't allowed to touch her. The garden seat was on the unit manager's desk. He glanced at it and then back at Scarlet. 'Is this what you wanted to show me?'

'Yes,' she said, and her voice shook. She cleared her throat. 'Um. It's a waterproof birthing stool.'

He looked at it again and realised that what she'd said was true. 'I see that now.' He was back under control and he could concentrate on what she was saying. 'What is it you want to do with it or maybe I don't want to know?'

She smiled and the force of it slipped in under his

rib cage. 'Don't be like that, Sinclair.' She had herself in hand as well, he could tell.

He just wished he didn't feel so shattered from that one touch. He tried to maintain concentration on the stool—a stool he wasn't interested in at that moment.

'So?' he said.

'So I want to use it here, and I'd like your support.'

He opened his mouth to comment but she held up her hand.

'Stop. Don't say no until I've finished. Just listen for a minute.' Her lips tilted and she smiled that devastating smile he remembered from their first night.

He could almost agree to anything if she looked at him like that again. He refocussed. He needed to get a grip here. He must be still off balance from Michelle's bombshell about Scarlet's husband.

She was talking and he tried to concentrate. 'Since I spent time at the valley community, I've really learnt to appreciate the difference made when a labouring woman is coping in the position of her choice. When she feels in control.'

She gestured to the stool. 'Whether it's in the bath, or a shower chair or a birthing stool. It takes a little getting used to when the woman's pelvis isn't in the position we're familiar with, but the results are worth the effort. I'd like you to agree to a trial of the stool until you see what I mean.'

'So the trial goes on until I agree—is that what you're saying?' Sinclair queried.

She laughed and the contagious sound made his lips twitch.

The humour was still in her voice when she spoke. 'It did sound a bit like that but that's not what I meant.'

'Really? Could have fooled me.' He was smiling, too. Of course he'd agree. He had no choice, in fact. He couldn't think of a good reason to deny the request, and if the women liked it, and the infection control people were happy, then he'd agree.

Who knew? Even Scarlet might be appreciative.

He patted the stool. 'One month. Then we'll have a ward meeting and see what the general consensus is.'

Her eyes lit up and he pressed his advantage. 'On one condition.'

Scarlet couldn't believe he was putting a condition on this. She put her hands on her hips. 'What condition?'

'You have to come and have dinner with me and tell me about your time in the valley.'

Scarlet's mouth went dry. That wasn't what she'd expected. She'd thought he might have insisted on being present when the women were on the stool or something equally cautious. But to ask her out. He'd said he wanted to hear about the community but just the two of them? She couldn't do it.

She could see it now. 'That would give the gossips something to talk about.'

He shrugged his shoulders. 'Is that your biggest fear? The gossips talking about us? My father would be in the house. Even your husband couldn't complain about that.'

Thank you for the reminder about 'Gerry'. That's another good reason why not, she thought. But it wasn't a good time to tell him she'd decided the marriage was finished. 'I'm sure he wouldn't like it.'

Sinclair started to turn away. 'I thought you wanted to promote your ideas on natural birth?'

Salvation came. 'I can't. I'm away from Cameron when I'm at work, I don't like to leave him when I'm home. I certainly wouldn't expect my mother to mind him when I'm not working.'

Sinclair wasn't fazed. 'No problem. Bring him with you. I'll get my housekeeper to prepare the meal before she goes home—she loves organising dinner parties. We'll go to my house and Cameron will be fine. I'll pick you both up at seven tomorrow evening.'

'Tomorrow?' Scarlet realised she'd squeaked as soon as the words left her mouth.

His face remained serious. 'That's the condition. Let me know if you can't make it or I'll see you then.' She watched him turn the handle and open the door.

She could smell a rat. Scarlet searched for signs that he was pleased with himself now that he'd outmanoeuvred her, but his face was expressionless.

'You'll need a bolt in your car for Cameron's baby capsule. As long as Cameron can come, we'll be there.' This might not be all bad. At least she'd have a chance to promote her views on the changes she had in mind for Southside. 'You could be sorry you invited us,' she warned.

He stood back to allow her to precede him from the room. 'I'll take that risk.'

Michelle was sitting at the desk and glanced up at them.

Sinclair rattled the keys in his pocket. 'Bye, ladies.'

Michelle said, 'Bye.'

Scarlet said nothing and Sinclair whistled as he went down the steps.

Neither woman said anything until Michelle looked across at her friend. 'He looks pretty happy for a man who's agreed to a newfangled idea.'

'What makes you think he agreed?' Scarlet said sourly.

Michelle blinked. 'Didn't he? I can't imagine that he wouldn't. He's always been fair and he hasn't got a closed mind like some. Now, his father I could understand. You must be slipping.'

Scarlet half laughed. 'You're right. He agreed to a month's trial.'

'So why the glum look? I'm confused. I thought you'd be jumping for joy with a new toy to play with.'

Scarlet slumped back in the chair. 'You're right again. I am pleased. I've just got something else on my mind. Do you want the nursery or the birthing suites?'

'Nice of you to offer, seeing as there's no one in labour,' Michelle teased. 'I'll take the mother-crafting on the floor. There's Karen's baby with meconium aspiration in the nursery. He'll keep you busy.'

Scarlet stood up and turned towards the nursery door. 'I need busy at the moment. See you later.'

Baby Wilson's X-rays were clipped up in front of the X-ray light.

Scarlet could see the two dark areas that indicated poor lung function. She moved over to the crib and stared down at the tiny infant. He had barely any hair and it made him look even smaller. 'Hello, Toby. Poor little fellow. I bet your mum misses having you with her in the room, though you are getting better.'

She checked the site of insertion of the intravenous cannula. His heart leads appeared secure and his heart rate and respirations were stable, although a little faster than normal. She changed the pulse oximeter clamp from one foot to the other to ensure the reading of his oxygen saturation was true.

Oxygen, measured and mixed with air, hissed into his Perspex head box and she checked the water levels and temperatures on the humidifier. He was getting it moist and warm.

It was a bit like painting the harbour bridge. By the time you finished all the hourly observations and tasks it was time to start again. Karen hobbled in and when she saw Scarlet her eyes filled with tears.

Scarlet held out her arms and the young woman buried her head in Scarlet's shoulder.

'I hate it here. I don't understand why Toby is sick. They all told me but I just can't seem to understand.'

Scarlet squeezed Karen's shoulder and sat her carefully in the chair before crouching down beside her.

'Hey, it's normal to feel like that. Do you want me to try and explain it again?'

Karen nodded.

'OK.' Scarlet grabbed a footstool and sat beside Karen, facing the crib so she could watch Toby.

'At birth, babies who have passed a bowel motion, called meconium, inside Mum's uterus have their mouths sucked out as soon as possible after birth. We use a thin tube to try and prevent the baby breathing in the meconium otherwise they could breath in meconium and gum up sections of the lungs, which leads to breathing problems, pneumonia and even worse.

'Unfortunately, sometimes there's already meconium inside the lungs.' Scarlet paused to see if Karen understood that much.

'That's what the doctor said, but how could it get in there if the baby hadn't breathed yet?' She wiped her nose with a tissue as she looked at her baby behind the Perspex wall of the crib.

Scarlet gestured with her hands. 'In normal circumstances, unborn babies have a shallow and rapid respiratory movement as they float inside their mother and lung fluid flows through their lungs.

'If, like your baby, something happens to cut down on the oxygen received, the foetus conserves energy by stopping these movements. Unfortunately, if the lack of oxygen continues, these gentle movements are replaced by deep gasping underwater breaths.'

Karen nodded her head as Scarlet mimed the breath movements.

'The foetal lung fluid is replaced by gasped contaminated amniotic fluid.'

Karen nodded.

'OK. So stressed babies, like Toby was after your bleed, often have meconium floating in the amniotic fluid. At birth, breathing difficulties are caused by the globs of meconium, which stop air entering the tiny tubes in the lungs, and inflammation is caused by the chemicals in the meconium that damage lung tissue.' She looked at Karen. 'Is that clearer?'

Karen nodded. 'So how long does Toby have to stay in there?'

'Until his breathing doesn't speed up when there's no extra oxygen added to the air. Luckily he only has a few small, inflamed areas and he's getting better all the time. Probably a few more days and he'll be able to come out. If he'd been much sicker we would have had to send him away to a larger neonatal intensive care unit.'

'I feel so lost without a baby like the other mothers, and I miss George.'

Scarlet squeezed Karen's hand. 'That's normal too. You've been very brave. Just spend as much time down here as you can without making yourself too tired. Don't forget you had a big operation, too.'

The next seven hours flew and Scarlet explained all the leads and lines connected to Toby. She even encouraged Karen to hold the syringe barrel while the expressed breast milk was run into Toby's stomach. By the end of the shift Scarlet was tired but satisfied with Toby's progress and Karen looked much more at ease around her son's equipment.

But the downside of a busy shift was the leftover tension that accompanied her home. Scarlet lay in bed and contemplated the night lamp of diving dolphins that rotated in the corner of the room.

She couldn't help thinking of the evening with Sinclair looming on her horizon, and it wasn't surprising that she couldn't sleep. If she was honest, her insomnia was more Sinclair-related than work-related.

If she was going to be honest, she'd felt good talking to Sinclair today. Once she'd got over him touching her. The feeling created by that one finger he'd laid on her bottom lip had resonated around her body and stunned her into silence. It had coloured the rest of her day. It had brought back a million tiny memories of a night she'd tried to forget and hadn't been able to. Damn him.

Which brought her back to the sweet consequences of that night. Did any reason justify the fact that she'd lied to Sinclair about Cameron's paternity? Had she presumed too much that Sinclair would feel trapped by her and her son? What it all boiled down to— wasn't it time she got over her gossip phobia? Was she too obsessed about what people thought and said?

Scarlet twisted her pillow in confusion. Why was everything so complicated?

By the time she finally drifted off to sleep Cameron was ready for another feed and Scarlet couldn't face getting up to sit in the chair. She snuggled him into bed with her and she fed him with her eyes closed.

He was still there when she woke in the morning. The breast that he'd snacked on for the rest of the night felt as flat as a pancake and the other looked like a balloon.

She started to giggle. Whatever she wore tonight would look funny with breasts like this. Another giggle escaped and Cameron woke up.

She shifted him up onto her shoulder. 'Did you have a party last night, son? Look at your poor mummy's breasts.'

He burped so loudly it set Scarlet off again.

When she went down for breakfast she was still smiling. 'Morning, Mum.'

'You look like you're in a good mood today,' Vivienne remarked.

Scarlet's brow creased. Had she been that hard to live with? 'Why? Am I normally bad-tempered?'

Vivienne patted her shoulder and placed a cup of tea in front of her. 'Just weighed down with the worries of the world on your shoulders, that's all.' She sat down beside Scarlet at the table and pushed the cereal and milk towards her.

'So what brought on this lightening of your mood?'

'I've decided to lose my husband.'

Her mother shook her head. 'Poor Gerry-the-geologist. I never liked him anyway.' She met her daughter's eyes. 'What about Sinclair?'

'Sinclair is an unknown factor. I'm not ready to tell

him about Cameron but my wish for the day is that we can find some common ground and friendship tonight.' She told her mother about the birth stool and Sinclair's condition.

Vivienne looked sceptical. 'Friends don't lie to each other. So be careful what you wish for.'

By the end of the day, Scarlet's nerves were getting the better of her and she wasn't smiling any more. What on earth had possessed her to agree to go to Sinclair's house? She should have suggested they eat here at her mother's—at least she'd be safe. Wimp, she told herself.

'What are you wearing?' Vivienne came in and sat on Scarlet's bed while her daughter was riffling through her wardrobe.

'I thought maybe my black jeans and sweater.' At her mother's look she laughed. 'Just kidding. Seriously, whatever I wear needs buttons in case Cameron wants a feed.'

'Everything in that wardrobe seems either grey or brown. Don't you have any brighter clothes?' Vivienne's nose wrinkled.

Scarlet sighed. 'Sinclair wants to hear about the maternity care in the community. It's not a fashion parade.' She watched her mother poke around her wardrobe.

'What's that red material I can see in there?'

Scarlet tried unsuccessfully to bury the swathe of material back behind an overcoat. 'That dress has a lot to answer for.' She pulled out a blue-green shift in linen. The straight lines would be flattering and it buttoned from hem to neckline. 'What about this?'

'It's not frivolous but I like it.' Vivienne scrutinised it. 'It will crush, though.'

Scarlet shrugged. 'He can see me ironed and then deal with the wrinkles later.'

Vivienne stood up and held out her hand. 'Sounds like a marriage to me. Give it here and I'll press it while you dress Cameron. You've got thirty minutes before he arrives.'

Scarlet felt the sudden thump of her heart. She was acting like a nervous teenager on her first date, not a twenty-five-year-old mother. She didn't need this.

At the McPherson Family Practice, Sinclair paced the kitchen as the clock ticked slowly on the mantelpiece. The table was set upstairs. All he had to do was take the cold platters out of the fridge and the hot ones out of the oven when he needed them.

His father frowned. 'For goodness' sake, sit down. I had no idea you felt this way about Letty Robin.' Frank McPherson's voice at least stopped the pacing.

Sinclair paused to lean on the back of a chair. 'Her full name is Scarlet. We're just discussing changes in obstetric care.'

Frank's voice was stern. 'Of course.' The scepticism was clear in his voice. 'I thought she was married? I expected better of you, Sinclair. I have all the time in the world for her mother but young Letty has proved herself flighty this last year.'

His father shook his head. 'I understand she moved into that hippie commune and goodness knows what she got up to there.'

The corner of Sinclair's mouth twitched. 'The marriage didn't work out, and as for the community...' He grinned. 'People who live there aren't called hippies and they don't call them communes any more either, Dad.'

'Humph. Well, I wouldn't know about that. You do have a certain standard to uphold, Sinclair. The McPhersons have been doctors here for three generations and we've never had a bad word said against us.'

Sinclair grimaced. 'That makes us a boring lot, then, doesn't it?'

His father snorted and it turned into a laugh. 'Wish I'd thought of that answer when my father warned me off Scarlet's mother.'

The older man stood up, slapped his son on the back. 'Goodnight. I'm off to read the papers on my bed and you needn't think I'll disturb you. Be careful. Those Robins are dangerous birds.'

He grinned at his father's pun. 'It's not even seven o'clock. And what do you mean, Grandfather warned you off Vivienne Robin?'

'It was after your mother died. Vivienne was a good friend to me. More than that. But your grandfather didn't like it and I could never stand up to him. But that's all water under the bridge.'

Sinclair had a horrendous thought. 'Do you know who Scarlet's father was?' Sinclair held his breath.

'One of the town's best-kept secrets. But, yes, I do.' He ran his finger across his mouth, pretending to zip his lip and winked. 'It wasn't me. Wish it had been. But there you go. Goodnight, son.' Frank sailed off to bed, unaware that his son was frustrated by his answer but relieved all the same.

Sinclair sank down on the chair and his breath eased out as he listened to his father walk along the hallway to his downstairs flat. Thank God for that. He certainly didn't feel brotherly towards Scarlet.

His grandfather had been dead ten years and his

own mother at least twenty-five. He couldn't remember much about his mother except that she'd sung to him when he'd been little. His childhood had been rock solid with amenable housekeepers but now he came to think about it he couldn't picture even one instance when he'd seen his father out with a woman. It was a long time for a man to be without female companionship.

But, then, he himself hadn't stayed home that much to see. He'd had a fairly active social life, although none of the women he'd known had struck that special note with him—until Scarlet.

It hadn't been a musical note he'd heard that night—it had been the complete jazz band.

He glanced at his watch. Time to go.

CHAPTER SEVEN

SCARLET was waiting for Sinclair when he arrived. He'd been hoping she'd wear the red dress. Unfortunately, it looked like his estimate of his chances was spot on. She looked beautiful in the blue.

Scarlet was very businesslike. 'Did you get the bolt for the baby seat?'

Luckily he had. 'It's all ready. My housekeeper minds her grandson and she lent me hers.'

She bent down to pick up the contraption from the floor beside the door. 'Here's the seat. I'll bring Cameron out while you fit it to your car.' It was as if she wanted to get the evening over and done with. He couldn't decide whether she didn't want to come with him or was frightened. Neither was a good sign for the evening.

'Can I come in first and say hello to Vivienne?' He watched the changing expressions on her face as she battled with her obvious desire to say no. Finally she stepped aside and gestured him in.

'As you wish. She's in the kitchen.'

'Thank you.' He smiled at her and she sighed. Her shoulders loosened and she sent him a tentative smile of her own. 'I won't be a minute,' he reassured her.

Scarlet heard him greet her mother and the sound of laughter. She sighed again. She'd been more wound up than she'd realised. She tried a couple of soothing breaths and felt a little better. This was stupid. What did she have to be afraid of?

121

The voice inside her head was quick to answer. How about the only guy who has managed to break down your defences and who also has the power to claim half your son?

This was a bad idea.

Sinclair's voice came from beside her shoulder. 'Ready?'

She jumped and the pounding of her heart in her ears disorientated her. She stared at him for a moment and drew some reassurance from the kindness in his eyes.

His voice was soft. 'Did I startle you? I'm sorry.' He looked around. 'Where's Cameron?'

She glanced up the stairs. 'I'll just get him if you take the baby seat and that nappy bag beside it.'

'Done.' He touched her arm. 'I don't like to see you this nervous, Scarlet. I'll bring you home whenever you want. All right?'

When he was sweet he was deadly and she could feel herself soften towards him. 'You must think I'm an idiot. I'm just out of practice.'

'Didn't your husband take you out?' She could tell he wanted the words back as soon as he'd said them. At least she wasn't the only one who put their foot in it. She felt guilty in her lie and almost felt sorry for him but chose not to answer—that way she couldn't say the wrong thing. She wished she'd never started that charade—but it was for Cameron's protection. Not hers.

The trip was short, and in no time Sinclair had parked his car in the driveway.

He came around and opened her door and Scarlet realised she'd been sitting there, staring up at his home, dreading their time alone. But then she remem-

bered his father was there. She clutched the nappy
bag as she got out of the car.

'I'll carry Cameron up the stairs if you like,' he
said, and opened the rear door.

'No!' She realised she'd spoken sharply but it was
too late now. 'I'll take him, in case he wakes.'

Sinclair stood back for her to lift the capsule out
of the car. 'Give me the little bag, then, and I'll lead
the way.' That was all he said.

She followed him in through the entrance and even
in her nervous state she had to pause and admire the
beautiful lead-light panels each side of the heavy
door.

By the time they'd climbed the stairs, her arm was
aching from the weight of the capsule. She unobtrusively swapped arms to flex her cramped fingers, hoping he wouldn't notice after his offer. Of course he
did.

'Independence can be a pain sometimes, don't you
think?' There was a glimmer of amusement in his
eyes but she refused to bite.

'Where will I put him?'

'As I don't suppose you want to go into my room,
perhaps the guest room would be appropriate.' He
indicated a hallway at the end of the large open-plan
room and she followed him through.

By the time she'd settled a sleeping Cameron on
the bed, surrounded by pillows, Scarlet was starting
to feel more in control. After all, this was her big
chance to bend Sinclair's ear about natural birth in a
calm and sensible manner.

The table was set in one end of the huge dining-
lounge room with full-length windows taking advantage of their height over the river. The furnishings

were a little spartan and lacked a woman's touch. Scarlet could see the streetlights from across the river reflected in the water and somewhere a motorboat chugged upstream.

They stepped out onto the covered verandah, and the breeze felt good on her heated face. It was quite cool for a spring evening, with a hint of storm in the air, and after a few minutes, while he pointed out local landmarks, she was glad when Sinclair suggested they go back inside. He slid the glass door across behind them to stop the light breeze.

'It must be beautiful here in the summer.'

'It is. But the view inside is better at the moment.'

She'd never been one to consider herself good-looking but she couldn't help believing he found her so. It was in the way he looked at her. 'Thank you, kind sir,' she said lightly, but the comment made her nervous.

As if he realised it, he changed the subject. 'Would you like a drink? Or I have non-alcoholic wine.'

She concentrated on the question. 'Non-alcoholic, please.' She went over to the lounge to perch on the edge of the black leather.

Scarlet noted the lined bookshelves and the latest stereo equipment in the room. 'So, what do you do in the evenings when you're not attending births?'

He smiled and the tingle it gave her travelled all the way down to her toes. There should be a law against a smile like that. She almost missed his answer. 'I socialise and play squash, or listen to music. I'm very boring.' He passed her glass and their fingers brushed.

Startled, her eyes met his and looked away. She was starting to feel like she was sitting on a low-voltage electric fence, with Sinclair zapping her every couple of minutes. Yeah, right. 'Boring isn't a word I associate with you.'

There was a smile in his voice when he spoke. 'So tell me about your time at the community.'

She felt her shoulders relax slightly. This was safer ground and she gathered her thoughts. 'It was different to what I imagined it would be,' she said. 'My mother had friends who built the first house in the valley, and Mum spoke of it as a good place to find yourself. A place without prejudice.'

He sipped his own wine and wondered out loud, 'Can any place really be without prejudice?'

He offered her some pretzels and she considered her reply while she crunched. The salt was tangy on her tongue—or was it just that all her senses seemed hypersensitive in his company? 'Most community dwellers are reluctant to come down the mountain to a hospital to give birth—I suppose that could be a prejudice against conventional medicine—but I believe that's because they have faith in the birthing process.'

He frowned. 'What happens when it goes wrong? Like Karen's pregnancy?'

She tilted her head. 'How often do you see a case like placenta praevia? Once a year in our three hundred births, which would be once every ten years for the amount of home births we have around here. That's why it's so important to be non-judgmental when these clients come in. They have to be encouraged to come if they need help.'

'I can see that. But what if they still decide not to come?'

'Then they accept the outcome as the natural course

of birth.' She could see he didn't like that answer. She wasn't thrilled with it herself.

He shook his head. 'This is where I have a problem. In Karen's case, ultrasounds for all women effectively remove the risk of undiagnosed placenta praevia. Don't you think personal preference against ultrasound is a bit harsh on the child or mother that might have been saved?' He shook his head and muttered, 'Personally, I'd say it was criminal.'

Scarlet saw his point. 'Well, to be honest, that's my dilemma as well, although I would say "ill-informed", not "criminal". And that wasn't the case with Nina's client. Nina did everything right and actively encourages her ladies to have at least one ultrasound. But George is the only man Karen trusts and our radiographers are all men. She refused on those grounds. But besides Karen's case, I know women who did everything their obstetrician suggested, including ultrasound, then spent the whole pregnancy worried about a deformed baby. All because the ultrasound thought it picked up something that wasn't there to start with. There has to be a happy medium.'

'I'll buy that,' he acknowledged. 'But I could never accept a child's death as natural attrition.'

Scarlet spread her hands. 'Hospitals have their own tragedies and sometimes all the technology in the world won't save a baby. But apart from obvious high-risk pregnancies that require a doctor, most healthy women are capable of giving birth to healthy infants at home.'

Her stomach rumbled, probably more from nerves than hunger. Embarrassed, she looked up at him. He grinned and offered her another pretzel.

'You were saying?'

She searched for her train of thought. It had been important. Got it. 'Where the community women are enormously strong is in their beliefs. I've come to believe the power of the mind is undervalued in medicalised birth.'

She would have loved him to pick up on this concept but it was a hard one for the medical profession to take on board. Especially if, from a doctor's viewpoint, someone was going to sue you if you didn't interfere and something went wrong.

Scarlet could see Sinclair had major problems with mind over matter. He paced across the room before turning to face her. 'I don't get that. If the mother's pelvis is too small, no amount of thinking about it will make that baby fit through.'

Scarlet watched his face. 'Maybe not. But if the mother listens to her body and assumes the positions to encourage optimal presentation and position as the baby moves into the pelvis, she could possibly avoid the disproportion by presenting the baby's smallest diameter.'

He swirled the liquid in his glass and then looked down at her. 'Did you have any shoulder dystocia while you were up there?'

A shoulder dystocia was when a baby's shoulders became wedged in the mother's pelvis at birth, usually after the head was born and was a life-threatening emergency for the baby if it couldn't be dislodged. Scarlet met his eyes unflinchingly. 'About the same amount as we have in Southside, but with less traumatic outcomes.' The conversation was hotting up.

'So what did you do there that was different to

what we do here?' He was every inch the consultant as he disdainfully glared down at her.

Scarlet refused to be cowed and glared right back at him. 'Get her upright.' At Sinclair's look of disbelief she nodded her head. 'That's right. Standing! It is amazing to see what positions a woman's body will tell her to assume when a baby's shoulder is caught. I've seen women squat or kick their legs out sideways until the baby dislodged and was born. The mother is just as aware as we are that something isn't right. If we gave her the opportunity to assume the position her body tells her to adopt in this kind of crisis, maybe the morbidity would be reduced.'

He shook his head. 'Give me scientific data to back that up. That's a bizarre picture.'

She shrugged. 'The baby was fine.' She placed her empty glass on the table and leant back. It was important that he grasp this concept.

'The picture is no more bizarre than a woman on her back with her knees jammed into her chest, someone pushing on her stomach and someone else pulling her baby's head.'

His eyes were cold and steel grey now. 'That scenario is a very rare occurrence and only used in dire emergencies. Many a baby is alive because of it.'

'And to think it might not have been necessary even then is a scary thought for those it happened to. Isn't it?'

'Where do you get off? I studied for six years of medical school, worked as an obstetric registrar for four years and have been here as an obstetrician for the last five years.' He glared at her. 'So don't tell me that some hill woman knows how the mechanics of birth work better than I do.'

Scarlet tried to hold back the smile but wasn't very successful. 'Poor Sinclair. Of course she does. She's been there and experienced it. And if she has a choice between listening to a textbook or listening to her body, I hope she takes the body every time.'

Sinclair smiled back at her but it wasn't amused. 'Pul-lease. Next you'll say women have a collective race memory stretching back to Eve.'

'I'd forgotten about that.' She grinned and they both laughed. The tension eased and their eyes met for a moment in recognition of how heated the topic had become.

Scarlet patted her stomach. 'Perhaps you should feed me before we come to blows.' Her smile was sweet this time. 'One more thing, though. As a midwife, for the rare occasions when something does go wrong, it is nice to know where to find you.'

'Gee, thanks.' He rubbed his jaw and his own rueful grin appeared. 'That was a pretty spirited pre-dinner conversation. I think I may suffer from indigestion.'

Cameron let out a cry in the bedroom and Scarlet stood up. 'I warned you might regret inviting us. I'll leave you to sort out my dinner while I do the same for my son.'

'You really do want your food,' he teased. 'I'll be back with it soon.'

Scarlet watched him disappear down the stairs and she couldn't help a small smile. That had been exhilarating and obviously a conversation that would never have occurred on a ward round. She moved quickly through to the guest bedroom but Cameron had stopped crying and was staring at the ceiling.

'Hello, baby.'

His little face creased into a giant toothless smile as he saw his mother. She picked him up and cuddled him before putting back down to check his nappy. He had that warm and powdery baby smell that could weaken a mother's heart from ten paces.

She kissed the top of his head and carried him back to the lounge room, resettling herself on the lounge. Sinclair had already made one trip from the kitchen downstairs because there was a beautifully decorated garden salad in the middle of the table with rock-melon and kiwifruit around the edges. But no sign of Sinclair.

She positioned Cameron at her breast and closed her eyes for a minute. There was some very quiet jazz playing in the background and with a start she realised it was her CD. Hers and the band's! He'd bought it. She grinned. That meant they'd sold at least seven copies now.

She savoured the familiar notes of the saxophone but it felt strange, knowing it was her playing. For the first time since Cameron's birth she itched to play again. She grinned once more. He'd bought their CD!

Scarlet ran her finger down the side of Cameron's soft cheek and her lips curved yet again. She was enjoying herself.

Spirited conversation was something she'd discovered she had a knack for at the community. Without television or nightclubs, nightly musical jams and conversation took over for amusement in the evenings.

As a child and as Letty Robin of Southside Maternity, she'd shied from the limelight of being outspoken. But at the community it had been a free-for-all and the hilarious and sometimes heated discussions stood as some of her most treasured memories of her time there.

It was strange to feel that same animation with Sinclair here tonight. That explosive night they'd spent together, they hadn't talked much. After the first light kiss and spontaneous combustion, she'd been so blown away that conversation had been limited to the half-sentences and murmur of lovers. All night.

Scarlet's eyes flew open. It was as if she'd peered behind a closed door and been blinded by what she'd seen. Now was not a good time to go there. Never would be soon enough—or perhaps one last glimpse on her deathbed just to know that she'd lived, she mocked herself.

Sinclair's footsteps sounded on the stairs and his head and shoulders came into view. His smile twisted her stomach into a heavy lump that ached. He placed the crockery platter on the table with a flourish and then poured two glasses of water from the carafe. 'Dinner is served and, please, note the easy portions that can be managed one-handed.'

'It looks wonderful, Sinclair. I'll be there in a minute. Cameron's nearly finished.'

He hovered between her and the table. 'Would you like a glass of water while you feed him?' He handed her one.

Her tongue felt dry as she slid it over her lips. She nodded. 'How did you know?'

He stood up. He gave her an evil grin. 'I didn't. But I love it when you do that with your tongue.' He moistened his own lips.

She almost choked on the sip she took and Cameron lifted his head and looked around. Scarlet met her son's bright eyes.

'Your daddy is one sick puppy, Cameron.' Although softly spoken, the words reverberated around the room and nausea hit Scarlet as soon as she'd said them. It was too late to call them back.

There was a deathly silence in the room then the sound of Sinclair putting down his drink. Her hand began to shake and the water in the glass rocked and splashed against the sides and threatened to spill on the baby.

Sinclair's voice was like a blast from the arctic. 'What did you say?'

Scarlet swallowed the prickle of fear in her throat and tried to make her brain function. The water was splashing out of the glass. 'Take the glass, please.'

He reached across and took it and she could tell he'd been careful not to touch her. She put Cameron over her shoulder, fastened her dress one-handed then closed her eyes. When she opened them he was standing in front of her.

His grey eyes were icy and a muscle twitched at the corner of his mouth. In all the years she'd worked with him she'd never seen him in such a rage. The air seemed to vibrate around him.

It was all the more frightening because his voice was so quiet, like an icy breeze from outside the glass doors. 'What did you say?'

She wasn't ready for this but obviously her sub-conscious thought she was. Her voice shook and she tried to put off the moment of truth. She had a mental picture of him staring down at her as she sat below him. 'We must look like the snake and the mongoose.'

His lips thinned even more. 'Don't even think

about joking.' His voice was clipped and slightly louder. She flinched.

That shocked him even more. He stepped back a pace and then walked around the room once as if searching for control.

He grabbed a chair, plonked it in front of her and straddled it backwards, but his hands gripped the sides and his knuckles showed white. He lowered his voice. 'I'm sorry.' The muscle twitched again at the side of his mouth and his eyes pierced her. 'Tell me.'

Scarlet drew herself to sit upright with a deep breath, met his eyes and watched for the words to sink in. 'Cameron is your son. There is no husband— I made him up. You were the only one. I went to the valley after our night together and that was where I found out I was pregnant. The end.' Her shoulders dropped as she let the breath out. It was done.

For a moment he didn't say anything. But his reaction to her news was all there in his face. Incredulity, suspicion, wonder and finally anger.

Anger. She'd known it would come but she didn't care now. He had the truth and he could do what he wanted with it. She knew what she was going to do.

'How nice of you to mention I have a son.' His voice was cutting and he glared at her, shook his head, looked at Cameron and then back at her. He laughed harshly. 'I actually suspected it but stupidly convinced myself you wouldn't exclude me if that was so.' He shook his head again. 'Did it occur to you, at any stage, that I might be interested in the fact that Cameron was my child?'

She could see the pulse beating against the vein on his forehead. Cameron had one just like it.

Scarlet tried to stay calm. 'Being interested that

Cameron is your child and being interested in Cameron are two different things.'

His eyes flared at that. 'Oh, I see. Tried and convicted of being a bad father without a chance to state my own case. How democratic of you. Where do you get off, lady?' He snorted.

She gave her own harsh laugh and Cameron stiffened in her arms. She drew a deep breath and soothed him. Her voice lowered and she almost snarled. 'Democracy was the last thing on my mind. With your help, I managed to achieve the one thing I swore I would never inflict on a child of mine. Illegitimacy. I'm dealing with that in the best way I can.'

His eyes narrowed. 'So it's my fault for seducing you?'

'No.' She met his gaze unflinchingly. 'It's my fault for allowing myself to be seduced. And the thought of the whole town knowing you are his father and the fact that we aren't together are unpalatable for me. I will not have him ridiculed like that.'

He was incredulous. 'So how is that different with the bogus husband?'

Her voice was matter-of-fact. 'I'm going to kill him off.'

He laughed. Once. 'Priceless. I suppose I'm lucky you didn't try to kill *me* off.' His voice was full of sarcasm.

Scarlet could feel the tattered edges of her control slipping and her eyes were prickling. The roughness in her throat was getting worse and she had to get out of there. 'You said you would take us home when I wanted to go. I want to go home. Now.'

He straightened and drew a deep breath before looking down at his son in her arms. His expression was harder than she'd ever seen it. 'Perhaps it is the most sensible thing,' he bit out. 'I feel like strangling you at the moment.'

She'd truly alienated him now. But she would probably do the same thing again if she had to. She looked at the beautifully prepared meal. 'I'm sorry about the food,' she murmured as she stood up.

His eyes flared. 'Damn the food. I'm sorry for me—and what I've missed out with my son.'

Tears shone in her eyes. 'He's my son and I'll deny it was you.'

He flinched but was in control again. His hands sliced the air. 'Time out. We're both upset. I'll drop you home now and call around tomorrow.' He swept up her things and picked up his keys. He didn't offer to carry Cameron and it was a silent trip home.

He left her at her mother's door, his face impassive. 'Cameron is mine as well as yours—get used to it.'

She watched him drive away and her heart felt like a cold fist in her chest. She trailed up the stairs with the baby capsule and Cameron asleep in it. A roll of thunder followed by a flash of lightning that lit the windows seemed appropriate to her mood.

After Cameron was settled, she changed into her nightgown like an automaton. Her brain seemed stuck in a vacuum of inactivity. When she slid open the wardrobe door to hang her dress up, a sliver of red mocked her from the back of the wardrobe.

She hated that dress. She wrenched it off the hanger and screwed it up. Her arm rose to throw it in the waste-paper basket but she realised her mother would comment so she jammed it in the bottom of her tote bag to dispose of in a charity bin the next day.

How had she been so stupid to let Sinclair find out that way?

Sinclair stood on his balcony, watching the storm, until the small hours of the morning. The rail was cold under his fingers and the lightning flashed images out of the darkness at him. Like the images he held of Scarlet and now Cameron. A flash and then gone. All he'd dreamed of was there in front of him but somehow poisoned with Scarlet's insecurities.

If only he'd tried harder to find her. If only she'd told him she was pregnant. If only...

Pathetic words and an exercise in futility. How could he salvage his family from this mess? And he realised the more he thought of Scarlet and Cameron as his family, the more the idea seemed to jell.

He could sort it out. It was a mathematical equation that needed breaking down and he needed to leave the emotion out of it.

But it hurt that she hadn't trusted him enough to tell him. She'd excluded him from her pregnancy, and he winced when he remembered she'd ensured he hadn't been present at Cameron's birth. He felt the anger rise up again in his throat and he stamped it down. That memory would forever be missing and no amount of wishing could restore his presence at that special time.

The simple answer to all their problems was for him to marry Scarlet. Except that the walls she'd erected against him seemed insurmountable.

But he had one advantage—he could provide what was best for Cameron! The spin-off was that he could then care for Scarlet as well.

His first impulse was to demand she marry him. It

would end her concerns for Cameron's illegitimacy.
She wouldn't have to work. Naturally he could support his own family and Scarlet could care for their
son full time. Maybe he should present it to her like
that. As a trade-off.

He thought of his father. He'd be pleased once he'd
recovered from his shock at the unconventionality of
it. The grandchild he wanted was closer than the old
man realised.

But Sinclair didn't want to buy Scarlet's hand in
marriage—he wanted her to come to him with an
open heart and loving arms. And if he couldn't have
that? Then he'd take whatever he could get and worry
about the rest later.

He massaged his neck. Scarlet loving him might be
a dream but it was worth fighting for. He slid his hand
along the wet rail and the water splashed off in spurts.

The best news out of this whole disaster was the
removal of the fictitious husband as a rival.

She'd said he had been the only one and that was
one nightmare he could stop imagining. The thought
of her with another man had torn him apart.

He flicked the droplets off the rail again as the wind
changed and drove the rain in towards him under the
awning and he had to step back. It was time to go to
bed.

Today was the day he started to woo Scarlet.

When Scarlet woke next morning, she'd decided to
return to the valley. A couple of hours in Sinclair's
company and all she had tried to salvage lay in ruins
at her feet. She was pathetic around him and couldn't
even keep her damn mouth shut. She'd be a basket
case if she let him into her life.

The next thing he'd be saying was that she had to marry him, and then she could spend the rest of her life with people like Tessa harassing her son when no one could protect him. The gossips would say she'd trapped his father. She hated being such a wimp but she couldn't help it.

Cameron could grow up in the non-judgmental environment of the valley and she would help out as the second midwife. Maybe her mother would come with her. She shuddered to think what Vivienne was going to say about this mess.

The phone rang and she glared towards the stairs. If that was Sinclair she didn't want to talk to him.

'Scarlet?' Her mother's voice floated up the stairs. 'It's Leah. She says she's in labour.'

Scarlet dropped the brush she was punishing her hair with and sprinted down the stairs to take the phone from her mother. 'Leah. How're you going?'

'Hello. Scarlet?' Leah's voice was tremulous. 'I started contractions during the night and I'm driving down the mountain this morning. Crystal said the baby is still breech.'

'That's really brave of you, Leah. I believe it's the best for your baby to be born down here if he's coming bottom first. You'll be able to go home after a few hours if all goes well.'

Leah started to cry. 'My boyfriend, Josh, doesn't want me to come down. He and Crystal are angry I'm not birthing here. I'm driving myself down.'

Scarlet frowned. 'Surely Crystal wouldn't let you do that?'

There was no answer from Leah.

'What about one of the other women? Surely someone can come with you and drive?'

Leah's voice was faint. 'There's a tummy bug going around at the moment and everyone is either sick or busy.' She sniffed. 'I'll be fine. I'll ring you when I get up from the valley to the pass.'

'Do you want me to come up and get you? How strong are the contractions?'

'They're fine and I only get about three in half an hour. Could you meet me at the hospital when I get down from the mountain?'

'I'll be with you as soon as I can. Ring me from the pass and I'll come and pick you up. It only takes ten minutes to get down the mountain but those bends are hard to negotiate with a belly in the way. Promise?'

Scarlet could hear the relief in Leah's voice. Scarlet fumed. How dare Crystal let Leah drive herself? She couldn't help the prickle of foreboding that gnawed in her stomach.

Crackling interference interrupted Leah's voice. 'I promise.'

'OK, I'll hear from you soon.' Scarlet put the phone down and went through to the kitchen to see her mother.

Vivienne looked up from the dough she was rolling. Flour hung in the air like fine mist.

'Mum, Leah is in labour and I'm meeting her up at the pass to drive her down. Her baby's still breech so she's coming in to Southside for the birth.'

Vivienne put down the rolling pin and brushed a strand of hair off her face. A white trail crossed her cheek. 'Will you leave Cameron here?'

'I'd like to, if that's OK. I'll feed him before I go, and if I get held up at the hospital there's a heap of frozen breast milk in bottles in the freezer. I'll worry about supplies for work when I get back.'

'That's sensible. The rain's stopped but there's another storm front coming, so be careful.'

Scarlet glanced out the window and noticed the thick, dark clouds moving their way.

'Just what we need. Why do babies like being born in storms?'

'It's nature. You were born in a storm.'

Scarlet tilted her head and looked at her calm and wonderful mother. 'I love you.'

Vivienne looked up in pleased surprise. 'Thank you, darling, and I love you.'

Scarlet shook her head. 'I never asked about my birth. When I come home I'd like to hear about it.' The distant sound of thunder rumbled along the valley. 'I'd better get Cameron fed and be on my way.'

She sprinted up the stairs and into the nursery. Cameron was asleep. 'Sorry, old mate. Have to wake you for this one.' She unwrapped him from his muslin sheet and checked his nappy. Cameron's eyes opened and he blinked owlishly at her. She dropped a kiss on his forehead and carried him across to the rocking chair.

It was then that she realised Sinclair was coming this morning. She wouldn't be home. Her absence left Cameron and her mother to face him. She sighed. There was nothing she could do about it but the timing couldn't have been worse.

Or better, if she wanted to avoid him. Her mother and Sinclair would probably think they had it all worked out by the time she came back. They'd realise their mistake.

By the time she was ready to leave, fat raindrops

were flicking against the window of the kitchen again. As she kissed her mother goodbye, the phone rang again. It was Leah and her fear was thick in her voice.

'Scarlet.' Leah sniffed and Scarlet could tell she was trying to pull her voice under control. 'The pains are down to three-minutely and I can't sit in the car any more. It's raining so hard and I'm scared.'

'It's all right, Leah. I'm on my way. Where are you?'

'I'm outside the Lookout Motor Inn in a phone box. The water is rushing down the road in the storm and I'm starting to get pressure.'

Scarlet winced. 'Stay in the car and I'll be there.' She slammed the phone back on the hook, grabbed her tote and her keys and tore out the door. Straight into Sinclair.

CHAPTER EIGHT

SINCLAIR grasped Scarlet's upper arms to stop her falling. 'Not so fast. I'm here to see you.'

She shook his hands off. 'Let me go.' Scarlet flicked her hair out of her eyes and stared wildly up at him. 'Follow me in your car. Leah's on the mountain and she's almost in second stage with a breech birth. I could do with your help. If you're coming, let's go!'

She didn't know if he followed but she didn't have the time to convince him if that's what he needed. But as she reversed out the driveway in her four-wheel-drive she saw his sporty car swing in a U-turn and wait at the gutter for her to go first.

That was the good news. She would have the best back-up person she could wish for at the delivery.

She peered through the foggy windscreen. How tragic that in the interests of safety she'd placed Leah in more danger than if she'd had her baby in the community with Crystal. If anything happened to Leah or the baby, Scarlet would never forgive herself.

She glanced back over her shoulder to the floor beside the rear seat. Her delivery set was there beside where she'd thrown her tote bag. She'd been caught without delivery equipment once before, and now it stayed in the back just in case.

Sinclair had opted for headlights behind her and she switched her own on. The windscreen-wipers were working as fast as they could but visibility was

down to a few feet. She hoped Sinclair knew the road
as well as she did.

It was a tense drive around the bends and already
the waterfalls had started at the side of the road. The
gutters were full and overflowing onto the tarmac,
narrowing the road even more.

There was no traffic in front of her so it only took
fifteen minutes. It probably should have taken twenty-
five in the conditions and she'd lost sight of Sinclair
a few bends back. Scarlet ground the big car to a halt
beside the telephone booth and she saw the shape of
Leah still shut in the booth.

Scarlet grabbed her bag and when she opened the
car door she was drenched before she'd crossed the
few feet to the booth. The fear in Leah's eyes as she
opened the door was a sight Scarlet would never forget.

Leah fired herself into her friend's arms and sobbed
into her shoulder. 'I had to stand up. I couldn't sit in
the car.'

'Good girl. You and baby will be fine.' The headlights of Sinclair's car appeared around the final bend
and Scarlet heaved a sigh of relief. 'Look. I've even
brought Dr McPherson to help.'

'Here comes another one.' Leah grunted and
swayed in Scarlet's arms. Sinclair got out of his car
with an umbrella and splashed through the water towards them.

Later she would remember that picture of him,
calm, dry and unflappable.

'She's in second stage. I don't think she'll make it
far and we need to get somewhere dry.'

'Get her in my car and we'll book into the motel.'
He opened the back door and held the umbrella over

Leah with one hand and pulled his mobile phone out with the other. He pointed to the sign advertising the motel, complete with phone number. 'I'd say every minute counts.' He spoke briefly into the phone as Scarlet helped Leah across into the back of the car.

By the time they'd pulled up at the office a woman with her own umbrella was signalling them towards a room.

'I'm Marie Peters. Call me Mrs P. This way.'

A man hurried towards them with an electric kettle and Scarlet had to swallow the bubble of slightly hysterical laughter as she realised what he was doing. Everybody had seen the movies and knew you needed boiling water to have a baby. She met Sinclair's eyes and a brief amused look passed between them as they helped Leah out.

By the time they were in the room, Mrs P. had whipped off the quilt and thrown a large plastic sheet over the bed and covered it with towels.

'I'm not lying down!' Leah shook her head and Scarlet squeezed her hand.

'That's fine, Leah. How about you squat up here and we'll put two chairs either side of the bed for you to hold onto? That way we can see how far baby's come down.'

Leah nodded, reefed off her sarong and her underpants and grunted and groaned as she crawled up onto the bed to heave herself into a squat. In that position, between Leah's legs could be seen a tiny bulge of baby's bottom and a tiny swinging scrotum. Mrs P. took one look, snatched the boiling water off her husband and ushered him to the door.

'Out,' she said. She turned back to Sinclair. 'What do you need?'

He looked at Scarlet.

Scarlet was calm now. The worst hadn't happened and she needed to salvage this moment for Leah. 'Some facecloths and hand towels would be great, thanks.'

Mrs P. opened the door, fired an order and shut it again. Then she moved up to stand beside Leah's shoulder for support. 'Squeeze my hand, sweetie, if you need to.'

Someone knocked on the door and the woman hurried over, took the hand towels and shut the door again before standing back beside Leah.

Sinclair threw his jacket on the dresser, rolled up his sleeves and went to stand on Leah's other side. 'Well, Leah. Of all the breech positions, frank breech is my favourite. Baby has his legs up around his neck and he's going to come out beautifully. Would you rather Scarlet helped him into the world?'

Scarlet flashed a look at him, unable to believe he wasn't going to insist on doing the delivery himself. It seemed like hours since she'd pulled up at the phonebox, fearing Leah would have her baby in the rain.

Leah nodded and Scarlet wasn't going to let the opportunity slip by. She'd only delivered half a dozen breeches, but the concept was the same. Let the mother and baby do the work, and beware of the head delivering too fast.

She undid the knot on her delivery pack and the sheeting rolled out to reveal a tiny plastic mouth sucker, a dish for the placenta, two cord clamps and a pair of scissors. She moved another tied roll aside for use later if needed.

Sinclair was ever practical. 'Do you have gloves in

that bundle of tricks on the table? Perhaps you'd better get them on.'

She wasn't touching anything until the last moment so Scarlet ignored him. 'How're you doing, Leah? You're pushing beautifully. Did we mention this child is a teapot with a spout? This is the only time we get to see what it is before we see who it is.'

Leah smiled up at Scarlet. 'So he's a boy.'

'Yep. No doubt about that. Why don't you have a feel?'

Leah snaked her hand down and tentatively felt between her legs. 'Oh wow. Two little cheeks and some boy parts.' Her eyes widened. 'Here comes another contraction.' She bore down steadily.

Scarlet slipped her gloves on and watched the buttocks elongate to include the tops of the baby's legs, then the knees on either side of baby's trunk. She didn't need to do anything yet and watched the buttocks and trunk deliver onto the bed. Once the legs were clear, the two little feet flopped down to hang in their intended position.

'Just arms and head to go. Leah, you're doing so well. I'll just catch his little arms so that they're born before his head.' Scarlet slipped her finger in beside the baby's chest, hooked one elbow down and out and then the other so that the entire baby had been born except for the head.

She allowed the weight of the baby to encourage its own birth until baby's neck was clearly in view. Then she supported the baby's body on the palm of her hand and the inner surface of her arm to ensure delivery of the head was slow and steady.

'It's really stinging,' Leah panted.

Scarlet looked up at Mrs P. whose eyes were like two dinner plates. Scarlet flashed a grin at her.

'I know. You're nearly there. Baby's head is the tough part. Little breaths and let gravity do most of it. We like to see baby's head born nice and slow for this part because he's had a quick trip through the pelvis and hasn't had a chance to change shape for the journey.'

Baby's chin showed first and then nose, eyes and forehead. Scarlet concentrated on preventing the back of the head from coming out too fast. 'Little panting breaths now, Leah,' she murmured.

Finally the entire baby was lying on the bed below his mother. Leah reached down and stroked his arms and chest before she lifted him carefully to nestle him against her skin. He cried briefly before shoving his fist back in his mouth.

'Congratulations, Leah.' Sinclair's voice was deep with emotion and his eyes met Scarlet's across the bed. He nodded and she inclined her head at his approval. The warmth in his eyes heated her own cheeks.

The next half-hour saw Leah and baby Edward settled down for a well-earned rest. Scarlet cleaned and repacked her equipment for later sterilising. She shouldn't have been surprised when Sinclair offered to hold Edward.

She caught him tickling the baby's cheek to try and make him smile and the sting of tears made her blink. Edward turned his cheek and latched onto Sinclair's finger and he looked up at Scarlet and grinned.

He'd missed that with his own son, she admitted to herself. And she had been the one who'd decided that. Scarlet bit her lip and turned away to watch

Mrs P. bustle around as if she were the proud grand-mother. At least Leah seemed to welcome the cosseting.

Sinclair left soon after to see about rooms for himself and Scarlet and the rain continued to fall in sheets from the leaden sky. News had come through that the pass was closed for the night because of the risk of landslides.

Again Sinclair surprised her by being more philosophical than Scarlet had thought he would be.

'I'm happy not to move Leah and baby in this weather anyway,' he said. 'We'll just have to find something to do to kill the time.' Scarlet shot him a look from under her lashes and what she saw in his expression made the heat creep up her cheeks.

Sinclair handed Scarlet a key and some dry resort clothes from the motel supplies, and she unconsciously clutched them to her chest.

'On the house, I'm told.' He grinned at Mrs P.

'Thank you,' Scarlet said, but the proprietress dismissed the favour.

'You three have made my day,' she said, and smiled fondly down at baby Edward.

She shooed Scarlet and Sinclair out. 'If you two are happy with Leah medically, do you want to shower and change? There will be lunch on up at the restaurant soon. I'll get a tray myself for our little mother.'

Scarlet turned to Leah. 'Are you right with that?' Leah nodded without moving her eyes from her new son. Scarlet suppressed a sigh. There goes that excuse, she thought. She crouched down beside the bed. 'If you have any questions, you can phone me on my room number or the restaurant.' She checked her key. 'It's room nineteen, next door to you.'

'That's fine. Thank you for everything, and you, too, Dr McPherson.' Leah flashed a brief smile up at Scarlet and then returned to her new favourite pastime. She looked lovingly down at her baby.

'It certainly was stimulating. I'm glad we can all relax now.' Sinclair's smile was genuine as he looked at the doting mother. 'Let's go, Scarlet. Leave Leah and Edward in our landlady's capable hands.'

Half an hour later, Scarlet was showered and dressed in shorts and a motel T-shirt. She'd tipped out the contents of her tote bag for toiletries and the red dress lay scrunched beside the rest.

She glared at it. Was it a good omen or bad luck following her around?

She combed her hair and damp tendrils curled around her face. Now that her hair was short, it curled at the ends in rainy weather. It was certainly easier than long hair.

She looked longingly at the bed and wished she'd said she was too tired to eat. Last night's sleeplessness was catching up with her and the thought of lunching with Sinclair was becoming less attractive by the minute. Especially when she knew she had to tell him she was going back to the valley community.

In the end, lunch wasn't the ordeal she'd thought it would be. Sinclair must have decided to leave the serious discussion until later. They talked about Edward's birth, the road closure and the torrential rain and devoured delicious bowls of home-made tomato soup and crusty rolls. Within an hour they were standing outside Leah's room after looking in on the patient—both mother and baby were asleep.

It was Sinclair who suggested that an afternoon rest wouldn't go astray. Then he looked up, an arrested expression on his face. 'Will Cameron be all right? What about feeds?'

'I've stockpiled plenty in the freezer. I rang Mum before lunch and she doesn't expect me until tomorrow. He'll be more comfortable than I will,' Scarlet said.

Sinclair winced as he looked at her straining T-shirt. 'I'd forgotten about that. How will you manage?'

Scarlet laughed. 'Our trusty landlady has helped me there. Her daughter is a counsellor with Nursing Mothers and she left me some equipment.'

'The woman's a marvel.'

'I don't think she's had such an exciting day in her life.'

'Well, I could live without it,' he said dryly. 'I've booked the restaurant for dinner at six. We need to have that talk.'

Scarlet resisted the urge to make a rude gesture with her tongue but 'Oh goody' slipped out. Sinclair just looked at her from under his brows. There goes my chance of sleeping, she moaned silently.

To her surprise, though, she slept for two hours after going back to her room, and felt better for it once she shook off the sleepiness. After a prolonged visit to Leah and Edward, she still made it back to her own room with half an hour to spare until dinner.

Scarlet sighed. She and Sinclair did need to talk. Sinclair's response when he'd discovered Cameron was his son hadn't suggested lack of interest. She smiled grimly at the memory of Sinclair's face. It was time for her to face the fact that he did have some claim. But claim on her son—not on her. She could be doing Cameron more harm than good if she excluded his father from his life. And herself more harm than good if she didn't keep him at arm's length.

That was the rub. Sinclair would be a good father and that was something she'd never had. She had no right to deny Cameron his.

Which brought it back to her reasons for putting a wall up between Sinclair and herself. Was it fear of him taking over or fear of her welcoming that state of affairs? She sighed. He only had to touch her and she'd lose the plot.

Again her lips twitched. If she knew Sinclair and his effect on her, she wouldn't have any choice. The least she could do was listen to how he wanted to approach his involvement with Cameron.

Which brought her back to whether to iron the red dress or not. She'd been putting off the decision all afternoon.

The mist and torrential rain seemed to have settled to stay here on top of the mountain and it felt like they were marooned in a cloud. It wasn't the warmest dress but neither were the shorts and T-shirt. When she looked out of the bedroom windows, visibility was down to less than twenty feet where an impenetrable wall of mist and rain blocked out the magnificent vista she knew was there.

The feeling of isolation was dreamlike, as was the slither of the red dress over her shoulders as she dressed.

Good or bad omen, there was no denying the dress

was with her and looked better than the other choice for dinner.

Besides, she didn't have a white flag to wear.

The thought made her eyes flash. She wasn't surrendering, just reassessing the boundaries of their relationship, and she was going to do it from a position of strength. She remembered saying after Carrie and Jim's bathroom delivery, 'If I was trying to make you notice me you wouldn't have to ask me. You'd notice.'

When Sinclair knocked at Scarlet's door he didn't expect to be greeted by the woman of his dreams. But there she was.

Her short copper hair curled around her face and her long neck seemed to float, swanlike, out of the plunging red neckline. He almost gulped. He cleared his throat and dragged his eyes out of the deep valley between her straining breasts to meet her eyes.

'Wow.' He couldn't actually think of anything else to say at that precise moment until he saw the amused glint in her eye. He held up his hands. 'I admit I'm a sucker for that dress.'

'And I thought it was me you fancied.'

He shook his head. 'No. It's the dress.' But he bet she could tell he was lying. He couldn't believe that she was in a playful mood and he felt the first glimmer of hope that everything would turn out right. He'd spent the afternoon trying to decide on his approach to a subject she wouldn't discuss. But maybe she was ready? He hoped so. Enough time had been wasted.

He crooked his elbow and she tucked her arm

through his. 'So the rain slowed down for a change,' she said.

He enjoyed the feel of her walking next to him and faint drifts of soap and some exotic perfume that he wouldn't have associated with her teased his nose. She really was delicious.

He realised he hadn't answered as they covered the distance from the rooms to the restaurant. 'The council is worried about landslides on the Waterfall Way and the road's still out, at least until tomorrow.'

She shot him a sideways look under her lashes. 'Afraid I'll run away, Sinclair?'

He shrugged ruefully. 'It's happened to me before.'

Scarlet had to give him that. 'It seemed like the right thing to do at the time.'

Sinclair didn't comment, just squeezed her hand and opened the door of the restaurant for her to precede him.

The manager came up to them and immediately ushered them to their table opposite the crackling fire. Once drinks and menus were brought, silence fell between them.

The moment had arrived. Scarlet drew a deep breath, lifted her head and met his eyes. She'd done enough running and hiding.

'So, what is your side of the story, Sinclair?' She put her drink down on the tablecloth but her fingers tightened around the stem of the glass.

'My side?' A small humourless smile crooked at the side of his mouth. 'Well, I suppose I met this vision one night.' He smiled down at her. 'And she looked very much like you do tonight, except for a cloud of copper hair around her shoulders.'

Scarlet couldn't help touching the hair that curled

around her ears and her face warmed more from his obvious appreciation than the roaring fire in front of them.

'Anyway, it turned out I knew this woman but had never really seen her until that night. What transpired holds a very special place in my memory.'

The sincerity in his voice couldn't be denied and she blinked back the sting of tears in her eyes. If only they'd had a chance to talk and her damned inferiority complex had allowed her to be there when he'd woken the next day. But she'd done what she'd needed to do at the time and she still wasn't sure it hadn't been the right thing to do.

Almost as if reading her thoughts, he continued. 'But then I lost her the next day.'

He picked up his drink and finished what was in the glass. His voice hardened at the memory.

'Nine months later she turned up married and in labour. Something she said...' he met and held her eyes '...made me wonder if there was any way the baby could be mine. But then I assumed that if that was the case surely she would have told me.' He looked away. 'You didn't want to see me, which was understandable to me as you were a married woman, but there was definitely something fishy going on.' He looked back at her.

Scarlet winced, and he saw it.

'Exactly.' She saw him watch her grip tighten on the stem of her glass. 'Now we both know that Cameron is mine as well as yours and we both need to decide what's best in this situation. Don't you agree?'

Sinclair obviously planned to have a say in Cameron's future. She nodded. 'I agree.'

'Whatever we decide to do, I'd like there to be no more hiding or fabrication between us.' He reached out and put his fingers over hers on the glass. 'Do you think we could do that, Scarlet?'

His fingers were sending signals up her arm and she tried to shut the feeling out to keep her mind clear. 'We could try, for Cameron's sake.'

Sinclair took his fingers away, sat back and sighed. 'I'd hoped it would be for all our sakes, Scarlet.'

She rubbed her hand gently across the tablecloth. 'Look, I'm sorry. This is hard for me, too. In my defence, I've spent most of my life ensuring that I didn't make the same mistakes my mother made. One night with you and all that caution went out the window. Even you said you'd never *really* seen me before that night. How did I know if it would take another five years for you to notice me again?'

His gaze travelled over what he could see above the tablecloth and one eyebrow lifted in amusement. 'I would have noticed you.'

She tossed her head impatiently. 'I needed time to sort myself out. Especially when the person I worked so hard to be was no better than the original version. So why have I been kidding myself for so many years? I needed to live in my real skin and feel comfortable. And guess what? I like the Scarlet I am.'

He captured her fingers in his and stroked her palm. 'I like her, too. Very much. What do I have to do to make you realise that?'

The sensation from her hand held in his clouded her eyes with indecision. 'That's the part I'm having problems with. I'm not used to seeing myself as something positive in someone else's eyes. Even if that is because I've had a baby with them.'

He squeezed her hand as if to deny her comment. 'Scarlet.' His voice was stern now. 'If you hadn't had Cameron, I would still be trying to have this conversation with you.' He ran his other hand through his hair until a spike stood up crazily at his crown. She resisted the urge to straighten it. The silence lengthened and she sneaked a look at his expression to find that he was waiting for her attention again.

Her voice was more tentative than she'd intended. 'What about the gossip?'

He shrugged his shoulder impatiently. 'What about it? So the doctor and the midwife are human. Big deal. They'll see I'm besotted with you.' His eyes were warm and he continued to stroke her hand.

She looked up. 'Say that again.'

'What? That I'm besotted? I go to sleep at night and you're the last thought I have in my head. I dream about you. I wake up in the morning and my first thought is of you. The idea of you beside me when I go to sleep and wake up for the rest of my life is one hell of a thought—and that's where I'm heading with this.'

His beautiful eyes met hers and the love in them finally left her in no doubt of his feelings. 'I love you and I want you as my wife.'

She couldn't believe he'd said that. His whole argument backed up his statement and she felt like crying again.

Here was more than she had ever dreamed of, but the lost child within her refused to believe it. 'You love me and want to marry me?'

His voice was dry at her paltry response. 'Rather than an echo, I was hoping for something like you loved me and want to marry me.'

She sat back. 'Technically you haven't asked me.'

'Technicality is your strong point, young lady.' He took her hands in his and their eyes met.

He held her gaze. 'Will you marry me, Scarlet?'

She was so close to saying yes. But she couldn't do it. Look what had happened the last time she'd rushed into something with him. 'Let me think about it.' She watched disappointment cloud his eyes and almost wished the words back. But it was all too pat. He'd found out Cameron was his child and wanted to marry her the next day.

Scarlet felt like a parachutist sitting on the edge of her first jump. Sinclair was the parachute she had to trust or miss out on what could be an exhilarating ride through life. But the downside was that she'd die if the parachute failed her. She temporised. 'I know I'm alive when you're around. I've never been the same since that incredible night we had together but I need some time to get used to the idea you want to marry me.'

He narrowed his eyes for a moment and she wished she could read his mind. Suddenly he pushed aside the menu and rose to his feet. 'Come with me now and let me show you what you have to get used to.'

Before she knew it she'd placed the napkin from her lap carefully on the table and had stood up. 'Where are we going?'

He leant down and whispered in her ear. 'For a night of sin.' Scarlet closed her eyes briefly and fought with her conscience. His breath on her ear won. She needed another night to remember.

CHAPTER NINE

SINCLAIR slid his arm around Scarlet's shoulder as they walked the length of the long verandah back towards their rooms and she savoured his possessiveness. The lights glowed fuzzily yellow under the verandah roof then disappeared ahead and behind into the mist. Scarlet felt as if she were cocooned with Sinclair in their own world. She'd always associate the smell of fog and rain with this night.

He opened the door to his room without taking his arm from her shoulders.

'Did you think I might escape?' He only raised one eyebrow and she admitted to herself the unlikeliness of it. She was where she wanted to be at this moment. She looked around and her eyes widened. 'This room is huge.'

'And the bedroom is separate.' He grinned wryly. 'This is the honeymoon suite.'

She laughed at the irony. The curtains were shut and a comfy lounge and stereo filled one side of the room. She draped herself across one corner of the lounge in a vampish pose. 'You were very sure of yourself.' She could feel the heat from his gaze.

'No. It was wishful thinking. Now, come here.'

She felt his desire like a real thing and when she looked into his eyes she marvelled at the softness she saw in his face. Softness for her. A chill ran down her spine and she shivered. It was too good to be true.

Suddenly frightened of losing the moment, she

moved towards him with a new intensity. This time was too precious to waste. She circled him, feeling the power of the woman course through her the way only he could make it flow. With her red dress swirling out, she shifted seductively in front of him.

When he caught her in his arms and brushed her lips with his, in that first touch she melted and sighed. The memories and incandescent feelings came flooding back. The taste and scent and pressure of Sinclair had been missing from her life as if she had been living in monochrome and only Sinclair could turn on the colour.

His lips grazed her cheek, the corner of her chin and that soft spot on her neck beneath the jaw. The goose-flesh rose along her arms at the tender warmth of his breath on her skin. They were together at last.

'I adore you, Scarlet Robin, mother of my son.' She tried not to stiffen in his arms. It was as if he had to again stake his claim on Cameron and her. To remind her of the plans he'd made.

She was frightened again for a moment of how much she had to lose until the new, stronger Scarlet reached up with her arms to pull his face down to hers, push aside her doubts and kiss him back. She would have memories to take with her.

All the time they'd wasted suddenly exploded into a volcanic need. His hands slid up her thighs and down again with a controlled urgency. Her need to feel him in her was so great and, combined with that eerie premonition, she whispered, 'I'll die if you don't take me here and now.' Unashamed, she pulled away from him to kick off her pants.

When she went to step out of the dress, he shook

his head and whispered 'Please, leave it for the moment.'

In a frantic shuffle of clothing beneath a scorching melding of their mouths there was no barrier between them except for the red dress and his shirt.

Suddenly he swept her into his arms and her feet left the ground as he twirled her once so that the ceiling spun above her. 'I can't believe I finally have you back in my arms. You taste beautiful, you look beautiful.' He bent his head to brush her neck and the valley between her breasts with his nose as he breathed in her scent. 'And it's been too long.' He hugged her and the sudden deepening in his voice sent quivers of anticipation flushing across her skin.

Scarlet's dress bunched around his strong forearms as he lifted the hem of it to bare her back and she felt the rush of warmth of her own readiness to welcome him. He cupped her buttocks firmly in his hands.

With hungry lips and anxious hands they poured the fears and frustrations of the time they'd lost into the communication of their bodies until he lifted her with intent and she answered his need by twining her legs around his body.

She felt his muscular thighs bunch against hers as he carried her like a limpet the few steps to the wall opposite and the cool surface of the plaster against her bare bottom only accentuated the heat and maleness that pressed against her belly. His chest and arms and flat stomach were hard against her as he lifted her one last time.

When he entered her she met his lips with hers and he muffled her cry with his mouth as they ground together in a mad, primitive coupling that went on and on and welded them in a hot, fiery place that seemed to shimmer so brightly it was almost too much.

Slowly the world returned to a calmer place and his hands gently massaged her buttocks as she quivered in his grasp. He brushed his lips down her cheeks and kissed her hair as they both struggled for breath.

He searched her face in sudden concern. 'I'm sorry,' Sinclair said. 'That was more unrestrained than I intended. You drive me insane. Did I hurt you?'

'No, no.' She soothed him back and uncurled her toes as the last shudders flowed like molten lava through her body. Scarlet felt like all the bones in her body had melted away.

He smiled. 'Let's not leave it so long next time.'

They leant quietly against the wall for a moment to catch their breath.

'My bottom is getting cold!' Scarlet whispered, and they both smiled, slightly embarrassed, and shook their heads at such wild abandon.

He carried her through to the bedroom as if she were very precious, and she snuggled against him.

'I love you,' she mouthed silently into the darkness so that he couldn't hear.

The bedroom curtains were closed and a small lamp glowed in the corner to welcome them. The room was dim and warm and the noise of the rain outside made it even more private.

Sinclair stood her gently beside the huge colonial bed and they both smiled at the mirrors on the ceiling.

He shucked his shirt off. 'You still have way too many clothes on.' His voice fanned in her ear as he slid the rest of her dress down her body. Scarlet shivered at the feathery sensation. She remembered that other time.

Scarlet lifted her hands to lay them above his heart and feel the pounding beneath his skin. She buried her nose in his chest. The tang of the distinctive aftershave she would always associate with him teased her memory. Tiny whirls of springy hair tickled her nose and she couldn't resist a tiny taste with the tip of her tongue. He shuddered. Delighted, Scarlet slid her tongue across his chest from one side to the other, nibbling and sucking until he held her head still and firm against his chest as he shuddered to control himself.

'You drive me crazy. Did I say that?' His voice was gravelly with desire and she lifted her head to meet his lips.

'Yes, but I'm glad.' She opened her mouth and merged with his warm breath, lips gliding and meeting and duelling with his tongue in erotic mindlessness for long intimate tastings.

When they moved apart, their breathing was audible even over the noise of the rain outside and they both laughed gently. It was as if they were suspended in time.

Suddenly, Sinclair moved to cup her buttocks again and he pulled her hard against his naked lower body once as if to reassure himself she was still there. His strong hands slid up to massage her shoulders in slow strokes that made her arch her back towards him. 'Your skin feels beautiful,' he murmured, and bent his head to capture one aching nipple in his mouth.

She moaned at the pleasurable pain and he soothed her with gentleness before reaching behind himself to flip back the frilly quilt so that he could sit her on his lap, facing him. With infinite care he caressed her other breast before returning to her lips.

From that point on their joining flowed like mercury, a ball of silver longings, rolling together and seamless in forming one molten entity that swept them away again and again until even their murmuring stopped and they fell asleep in each other's arms.

When Sinclair woke after midnight, Scarlet was gone.

His stomach dropped and he tightened his hand on the bedhead. He couldn't believe she would do it again. He slid from beneath the sheets and checked the bathroom and lounge room. Both rooms were empty.

Where could she go?

Then, in the distance, he heard a baby cry and he realised she would be with Leah.

He sighed. Today he would find out about the shortest length of time it took to get legally married and start leaning on her for a decision. He couldn't take the strain of wondering if she would disappear again.

He sat back on the bed and picked up her pillow. When he inhaled her scent from where her head had lain, he smiled. He'd wait for her to come back.

In the morning, the rain had cleared and they shared their first sunrise together. Sinclair filled the spa with hot water and bubbles and carried her, laughing and kicking, into the water. Scarlet found that washing him was a delightful occupation.

'There's something special about a bath big enough for two people,' Sinclair murmured afterwards, and Scarlet grinned.

'We should get one for the maternity ward. This would be ideal for our water births, you know.'

He groaned. 'Get me the protocol first. I can see a

lot of changes in the next year. I think we should have another baby to give me some rest at work.'

Scarlet stiffened and wouldn't meet his eyes. She slid from the water and wrapped herself in a towel. 'I have to see how Leah is doing. Crystal is coming for her at eight.' She tried for lightness. 'I'm starving. Why do you think that is, Dr McPherson?'

Sinclair rolled over in the water. 'Come here and I'll feed your hunger.'

'Is that what you're going to do every time I don't instantly agree to your plans? Drag me off to bed?'

'Give me a break.' He reached over and tried to grab her ankle. 'I've been celibate since November.'

Scarlet narrowed her eyes. That reminded her. There was something else she'd have to clear up. 'What about the delectable Tessa? I hear you went out with her a few times and that she even considers you secretly engaged?'

Sinclair grinned, rolled back onto his back and put his arms behind his head. 'Jealous?'

'Should I be?' She watched him in the bathroom mirror and felt sick as she waited for the answer.

'No. I only ever dated Tessa a few times and nothing ever happened. We're certainly not engaged, secretly or otherwise.' The conviction in his voice made her shoulders sag in relief. She leant over and kissed him. 'Thank you for a wonderful night and morning.'

He ran his finger down her leg. 'Let's go home. I need an answer from you and I can't wait to see our son.'

Later that morning, after a phone call from Scarlet, Leah's repentent boyfriend had arrived with Crystal to take his family home.

'He's still in the sin bin,' Sinclair remarked as the youth's tentative apology was ignored by Leah.

Scarlet smiled at the term for football discipline. 'So he should be. But she'll allow herself to be worn down with some spoiling. They do love each other. Apparently his friends are partially responsible for his attitude—but he's a father now. His first loyalty is to Leah and Edward. She'll make sure he gets the point.'

'And if you say yes, do you think you'll train me, too, Scarlet Robin?' Sinclair's arm was strong around her shoulders and she stored another memory.

He was pushing and she was finding it harder to resist the urge to throw caution to the winds. He wasn't playing fair. Her voice was quiet. 'No matter what we decide, I'm sure we've both got some learning to do.'

As the two cars disappeared, Sinclair turned her to face him. 'Drive carefully. I nearly had a heart attack, following you up the mountain. You drove like a maniac.'

Scarlet planted her hands on her hips. 'How can I drive like maniac when I drive an old Landcruiser? We plod along.'

'Well, if that's plodding, stick to a crawl. I'm going first so I know where you are.' His voice was dry.

'You're not earning yourself any brownie points by being dictatorial, you know!' She still had her hands on her hips.

He stepped forward and slid her hands down her waist with his own. 'It's only when I get scared I might lose you.'

She nearly said, You be careful, too.

Fifteen minutes later, as they started down the

treacherous mountain, she wished she had. The road had been open for an hour and freshly bulldozed landslides were heaped at the cliff side of the road. The road was full of slush and mud and Sinclair's car wasn't as happy wallowing in it as Scarlet's heavy Landcruiser was.

Water cascaded off the banks and every few feet small rocks bounced off the mountain. Scarlet had never seen it so wet or unstable. The Landcruiser ground down the hill steadily but Sinclair's car ahead slithered and slipped.

His driving was impeccable and showed a skill far greater than Scarlet's, but there was nothing he could do to avoid the sudden giving way of the cutting to his right. His red taillights flashed on as he braked and Scarlet's heart thumped in her chest.

For a moment she thought he might have stopped in time to avoid being sucked across the road by the rubble. But more bank gave way behind the first and a wave of mud and sticks and great tree trunks all came tumbling across the road in an inexorable wave that plucked up Sinclair's car like a toy and rolled it over the edge of the left bank towards the cliff edge.

Scarlet screamed and slammed on her own brakes and the Landcruiser stalled.

She didn't dare blink as she followed the flashes of Sinclair's car as it was rolled in the mud and huge branches until finally the mud monster sighed in one final heave and settled. The rear of Sinclair's car poked into the air about six feet from the edge of the cliff. The front half was submerged, and she tried to remember if the windows were up on his car. Apart from the risk of him suffocating, she knew that any shift of the earth again and the whole car was over the edge for sure.

With teeth chattering in shock, she inched her big car as close as she could get to the edge of the soil from the slide and pulled over. She jumped from the car only to end up ankle deep in thick mud and rubble, but she didn't feel the cuts to her feet as it scratched and tore off her thin sandals. She heard another car pull up behind her but ignored it as she fought to unhook her winch from the front of her bull bar. It was stiff and dry and needed maintenance it hadn't received since Cameron's birth.

She tore at it with her nails almost weeping with frustration.

The slosh and slurp of mud announced the arrival of others. She didn't turn around. 'There's a man buried in that car. We have to pull his car out before he dies.'

'Let me help, lady.' The big man behind her slid burly arms past her shoulder, worked the hook free and gave it to her. She ducked under his arm as he started to uncoil the winch line to give her slack. Scarlet slipped and slid with the line in her hand as she dragged it towards Sinclair's car.

She had shut down all thought except that if she hooked Sinclair's car to hers at least he couldn't go over the cliff. When she reached the car she wanted to drop the line and claw at the windows, but there was sanity in securing the line around the strongest point she could find. With that done, she turned to find the burly man at her shoulder.

'We'll try the rear door but gently goes, missus.'

Scarlet wiped a distracted hand muddily across her cheek and nodded. The car was sticking out of the mud like a thrown javelin; evidence of it having been rolled in the mud obscured any view inside.

The burly man heaved on the rear door and it creaked open a little until it jammed on a mound of mud. Scarlet fell to her knees beside the obstruction and clawed to make a dent deep enough to allow the door to open. Finally they could open it enough to see in.

All the windows were shut and no water or mud was in the car. Sinclair flopped against the restraining seat belt as he hung forward, unconscious, against the belt. Blood dripped slowly down his face. But he was breathing!

A sound of sirens came closer and the man pulled her back gently but firmly as Scarlet went to climb in.

'Just wait, lady.' She tugged against him but he wouldn't budge. 'They know how to move people without doing more damage.'

She sagged back, suddenly weary and frightened of doing more harm than good. 'You're right.' She could hear more people squelch closer through the mud and she stepped back out of the way.

She retreated to the edge of the mound and leant her back against a wet tree. Rivulets of water trickled down her back but she didn't feel them. She felt locked in a solitary nightmare as a group of yellow-coated emergency workers converged on Sinclair's car. They talked amongst themselves and discussed the best way to get Sinclair out, and she felt as if she were listening to a serial on the radio. Except that it was about someone she was terrified of losing.

'Good idea, the winch. But it could've pulled both cars over, I reckon,' one said.

'He's lucky it didn't fill up with water,' said another. 'Where's the ambulance guys?'

'Just pulling up now. I don't want to move the car until they've been in for a look.'

'We'll start digging this out and maybe it will sink back this way.'

Scarlet's teeth started to chatter again and she wrapped her arms around her stomach to stop the nausea that threatened to overwhelm her.

The burly man came up to her with an army blanket and pulled her away from the tree to throw it around her shoulders.

'You might be better in your car now it's getting busy around here.'

She gazed up at him as if to gain some idea of whether Sinclair would survive but, of course, he couldn't know. She looked down and allowed herself to be led back to her car.

'Thank you for your help.'

He squeezed her shoulder. 'You know him, don't you?'

She swallowed the lump in her throat. 'He asked me to marry him last night.'

The burly man opened her car door for her. 'Well, I hope you said yes.' Her eyes filled with tears.

The next hour dragged past and Scarlet felt a hundred years old by the time the ambulance pulled slowly away from the scene. They would transport Sinclair to the mountaintop and a helicopter would fly him to Northern Rivers Hospital. He hadn't regained consciousness and his face was the colour of white marble and just as still.

The burly man had vouched for her and she'd been

allowed to squeeze Sinclair's hand once and kiss him
on a part of his face not covered by the oxygen mask.
But the concern of his attendants hadn't encouraged
her to hold them up long and soon he was gone.

It was then that a sense of urgency set in. She had
to get home to Cameron and they needed to be at
Sinclair's side. She had this awful fear that if she
wasn't there to encourage him he might never wake
up.

The road to the valley below would be blocked for
days, and that meant she'd have to go back up the
mountain and further north to get down by a different
pass. She swung herself back into her car and reversed out of the quagmire and back onto the wet
road.

By the time she pulled into her mother's driveway
the tears were streaming, unchecked, down her
cheeks. Her mother was standing beside the car by
the time she opened her door.

'Thank goodness, you're safe. They said one person critically injured on the mountain and I rang the
motel. They said you'd left hours ago.'

Scarlet stepped wearily from the car into her
mother's arms. 'It's Sinclair. His car was caught in a
landslide and he's unconscious. I thought he was
dead. Where's Cameron?'

'Come inside and sit down.' Her mother looked her
up and down. 'On second thoughts, come in and have
a shower. You're saturated and covered in mud.' She
frowned at the streaks of blood on her daughter's feet
and the wild look in her eyes. 'I want to see your feet
after your shower, too.'

'I can't stay long. I've come to get Cameron and
I'm going to sit with Sinclair until he wakes up.'

Vivienne's voice was firm. 'You'll be no use to Sinclair if you're a physical wreck. I'll ring to check he's there safely, and I'll come with you and help with Cameron. Jump in the shower and I'll get some things together.'

By the time Scarlet came downstairs from her shower, Vivienne had packed a picnic basket of food and a large overnight case for the three of them. A plate of scrambled eggs sat on the table and Vivienne was sipping tea as she jiggled a solemn Cameron on her knee.

When he saw his mother his tiny face screwed up and he let out a loud wail as if to ask why she'd left him.

Scarlet scooped him up and buried his face against her neck and sniffed his sweet baby smell. 'Poor baby. Mummy's here.' She unbuttoned her shirt as she sat down and whistled at the bitter-sweet agony of overfilled breasts and Cameron's eagerness.

When she had her breath back, her eyes searched her mother's face. 'Is Sinclair all right? What did they say?'

'Not much. That he was in Intensive Care and still critical but stable at the moment. Eat your eggs and we'll go as soon as you finish Cameron's feed.'

Scarlet looked across at her mother. 'I love him, Mum. He asked me to marry him.'

Vivienne squeezed her daughter's hand. 'I hope you said yes.'

Scarlet shook her head and her heart ached for all the things she hadn't said. Having seen Sinclair lying there, so still and white as they'd taken him away from her, she realised what she might have lost because she'd been too weak to take a risk. She wished she could block out the idea that she might never have a chance to tell Sinclair all the things she wanted to, and tried to concentrate on normal things. 'How did you go with Cameron?'

'He was an angel. A little sad at times but took his bottles once he realised his favourite way of drinking wasn't going to happen. How did you cope with your poor breasts?'

'I managed. Which reminds me, the cold bag is in the car and I have to freeze the milk in there.' Her thoughts returned to Sinclair. 'Does his father know?'

'Yes. Poor Frank. Sinclair is all he's got.' Vivienne stood up as if she had to do something. 'I'll pack the car and lock the house.'

CHAPTER TEN

WHEN they arrived at the hospital Scarlet felt like an intruder in an alien world. The corridors were unfamiliar and the faces unknown, and she felt invisible in her fear that Sinclair wouldn't recover. It smelt like a hospital and that was something she never noticed when she went to work at Southside.

Vivienne pushed the pram while Scarlet scanned the corridor for signs to the intensive care unit. Her rubber soles squeaked on the linoleum. When they finally found the right ward, the thick frosted-glass doors were shut.

She pressed the bell for entry and it seemed hours before anyone came.

'Can I help you?' The tall blonde sister looked strained.

'I want to see Sinclair McPherson, a patient.'

'Are you immediate family?'

Scarlet felt like screaming, He's the father of my child, but what if Sinclair died? She couldn't do that to old Dr McPherson. Sinclair had an unblemished reputation.

'We're very good friends.' But she knew that wouldn't be good enough.

'I'm sorry. His condition remains critical and the specialist is with him at the moment. Perhaps you could take a seat out here. His father is with him. We'll let you know if there are any changes.'

Scarlet put her hand on the woman's arm as she

went to close the door. 'Is he conscious?' When the sister shook her head, Scarlet closed her eyes. She heard her mother's voice asking if they'd let Sinclair's father know that they were here, but it seemed to come from a long way away.

Scarlet sank down on the hard vinyl seat beside the door and felt like crying with frustration.

The sister was still talking to her mother but trying to edge away. 'Look, I'll try, but he's talking to the neurosurgeon and it's very busy in there.' Her smile was distracted and then she closed the door. They could see her shadow shrinking through the glass as she hurried back to what she'd been doing.

Scarlet felt her mother sit down beside her. 'She said a neurosurgeon. That doesn't sound good.'

'Sitting out here, with suppositions and scraps of information, is no good. So don't go imagining what you have no idea about,' Vivienne soothed. 'Where is Frank?'

As the words left her mouth the glass doors opened and Sinclair's father came out. He looked even older than usual. 'I'm here, Vivienne, and thank God you are, too.' He opened his arms and Vivienne went into them as if she belonged there. She hugged him and then stepped back.

She looked down at her daughter and grandson. 'They wouldn't let us in.'

He leant over and squeezed Scarlet's shoulder. 'Well, did he pop the question?'

Scarlet's eyes widened. 'You knew?'

'That Sinclair loves you and wanted Cameron to be his son more than anything in the world.' He smiled sadly. 'I hope you said yes.'

She bit her lip and then looked away. 'I will if I

get the chance.' He sat down beside her and slid his arm around her shoulder.

'Then you'd better get inside and tell him. Talk some sense into him. The longer he remains unconscious the bleaker it looks. There really is only room for one at a time in there. I'll stay with your mother and Cameron out here.' He rang the bell and the tall sister appeared again.

'This young woman is my son's fiancée. Please, give her some time with him.'

The walk from the glass doors to Sinclair's bed was the most frightening thing Scarlet had ever done. What if nothing she said or did could help Sinclair? She had to try for herself, for Cameron but mostly for the wonderful man that was Sinclair.

She thought of the power of the human mind—and all the births that had awed her because of the mental power of the women. As she came closer to the room she closed her eyes for a moment and drew a deep breath. If she could reach Sinclair's mind, who knew what they could accomplish? Hearing was thought to be the last sense to shut down in unconsciousness and if Sinclair could hear her then there was hope.

She eased into the room and looked down at the man she could finally admit she loved with all her heart. Now, when it was almost too late. Tessa and gossips and illegitimacy were all mere flyspecks on the window of life. The thought of losing Sinclair finally freed her from the fishbowl she'd swum around in for too long. Other people looking at her only mattered if she cared. What she cared about now was Sinclair and the life they should have had together.

'Oh, Sinclair,' she whispered. 'I'm sorry.'

The heart monitor leads criss-crossed across his chest like gaudy jewellery and his arms lay limply by his sides with intravenous fluids trickling into him in measured doses. The hiss of the ventilator had always made her uncomfortable but in this instance she acknowledged her relief that it helped Sinclair as it breathed for him.

There seemed so much extra equipment standing by in case it was needed.

She sank down in the chair beside him and wrapped all her fingers around his right hand. Where did she start?

'Sinclair. It's Scarlet here. I don't like to see you lying so still and quiet. You've always been larger than life to me.'

She leant over and stroked his face. There was a vivid graze across his right cheek and a purple bruise shadowed under one eye.

She thought back over the changes to her life in the last year since she'd come to love him.

'You know it was you and my response to you that I hid from all those years.' She sighed.

'It was a scary thing for me to realise that I could totally lose myself in you. But I've finally come to realise that really I grow when I'm with you and you grow with me. We're part of the same tree, Sinclair. A family tree that we've broadened to include Cameron.

'But I'm not afraid of that love I have for you now. It's a powerful love and I want to harness that power and use it to make you come back to me, Sinclair. I love you with all my heart and I need you to know that. You can't leave Cameron or me. We both need you. So wake up, my darling Sinclair. Wake up and smile at me.' She rested her forehead on his hand.

Scarlet heard the sister come in. She sent Scarlet a brief apologetic smile and busied herself with a round of observations that made Scarlet think of Toby in the crib the other day.

She searched Sinclair's face for any changes but his beautiful eyes remained hidden from her by his long lashes and his mouth was still.

Constrained by the other woman's presence, she found herself doing gentle reflexology massage on his palm and fingers, and it soothed her to go through the relaxation hand massage she'd learnt to give women in labour.

Once she thought she detected the smallest squeeze back from him but when she froze her movements there was no movement from the hand in hers. The excitement died in her chest and she sighed as she lifted his hand to slide it across her own cheek. The reserve she felt in the other woman's presence faded until she didn't notice her. All she could think of was that the man she loved was slipping away.

'We'll buy a strong, safe, family car. None of these little sporty numbers you like so much. Look how useless it was to protect you. I can see you in a big shiny silver Volvo sedan, Sunday driving with Cameron and I and maybe a little brother or sister for him in the back as well.'

She closed her eyes and laid her head down on the bed over his hand. 'But I need you in that picture, Sinclair. Wake up, my darling.'

But he didn't wake. Not that day or the next. The brain activity scan was inconclusive and there was some discussion on transferring Sinclair to Sydney to a more long-term facility.

Scarlet spent three nights snatching sleep in the sick relatives' section of the nurses' home, with Cameron sleeping in the pram in the room.

Cameron fretted more than normal as his baby antennae picked up the tension and fear from his mother and grandmother, and he'd cried the one time she'd sneaked him into the child-free zone of Intensive Care to see his father. Now, each time she visited, she booked him into the crèche. Her mother was busy enough looking after Sinclair's father.

She couldn't go home, had to be close to Sinclair in case he woke—but he didn't.

On the fifth day they would transfer him and she'd follow to Sydney. Scarlet stared blindly around the small, bare relative's room with the few comforts her mother had brought to soften her solitude and the bag of disposable nappies they'd resorted to using. She didn't even have a photo of Sinclair to put on the metal dresser.

She dashed away the weak tears and put the earphones of her portable CD player in her ears. In ten minutes she could go back again and sit with Sinclair. Maybe tonight…

Later as she followed the sister through the door of Intensive Care she bit her lip. Either she was getting paranoid or the doctors and nursing staff were avoiding her eyes. Dread sat like a vulture on her shoulder. Sinclair's father was in the room with Vivienne and they both stood to wait outside to allow her to take their place. Frank had aged more each day and even her mother was starting to look despairing of a miracle.

'Did you sleep, darling?' her mother asked.

'I closed my eyes. How is he?' She stood aside as they moved past her towards the door.

'No change.' Frank's voice was gruff and Scarlet saw her mother squeeze his shoulder in comfort. In his creased face, his eyes were suspiciously bright. Scarlet felt the tears prick in her own throat.

She watched them walk away before moving into the room to smile woodenly at the sister who'd just finished recording Sinclair's observations. The nurse smiled at a point just over Scarlet's left shoulder as she left the room.

Scarlet felt as if she were living in a lonely wind tunnel that was sucking the life out of her—and Sinclair. There had to be something she could do.

The chair felt warm where her mother had been sitting and she was grateful for that small comfort. She picked up Sinclair's hand and squeezed his fingers. His hands were limp beneath hers.

'What can I do to make you wake up, darling?' She stroked his fingers with her other hand and thought of the first night they'd been together.

That moment at the bar, when the drunk had grabbed her shoulder and Sinclair had appeared out of the crowd like a magnificent mirage. His gorgeous smile as he'd looked down at her had gone straight to her heart and had stayed there ever since. All the nerves she'd felt about playing for the audience had been nothing compared to her nervous response to Sinclair—her rescuer. She'd loved him for so long, and had hidden it from herself behind her façade of meekness. Tragically, there was so much they still didn't know about each other. There were so many things they had yet to share.

She thought of her saxophone, tucked away in its case at home. The tears started again when she realised that she might never be able to play just for Sinclair. She wiped her eyes and leant across to stroke his brow.

'I wish I could have played for you. I haven't played since just before Cameron was born. If anything happens to you I don't think I'll ever play again.' His eyes remained closed and her mind couldn't help bargaining with God and with Sinclair.

'If you wake up, we could sit on your verandah and I'd pour all the love I feel for you into the music. I'd play so that the notes would soar into the air and up and down the river until they found a home in the mountains or the sea.' She pictured them sitting there, on a summer evening, Cameron in Sinclair's arms as she played. She could almost feel the warm summer breeze on her face. 'I want to share that with you, my darling, as your wife. If only I hadn't been so scared. I should have said yes when you asked me. Please, give me another chance.'

The tears ran down her face and she dashed them away with a sniff. She wouldn't give up. When she rummaged in her bag for a tissue, she clucked impatiently as it became tangled in the headphone cord. The portable CD player her mother had brought and her own CD was in there. She unravelled the cord and drew it from her bag. He could hear that at least.

Scarlet looked up at the sister as she entered the room again. 'Is it all right if I put headphones on Sinclair to listen to some music?'

The sister looked surprised but agreed. 'It can't do any harm.'

Scarlet pulled out the Discman and set the controls—checking it wasn't too loud—before she slipped the headphone plugs into his ears. She watched his face carefully for any signs. There was no response, but what had she expected? At least she could play for him.

She sat back and took his hands again to start the gentle reflexology she had performed each day as he'd lain unconscious.

She would never give up. One day he would wake.

The first time his fingers moved in hers she froze and cautioned herself against false hope. The movement wasn't repeated and she rested her face against his hand. She must have imagined it.

The second time she felt Sinclair's finger move she knew it wasn't a dream. His knuckle had rubbed her cheek and she could feel the movement vibrate through her.

She lifted her head slowly and looked into his face. His eyes were open!

The world suddenly shone with more brightness than she knew how to cope with. The sister dropped her chart as she glanced across and saw his open eyes. She leant towards the door and called to other medical staff and suddenly the room was filled with people.

Her heart thumping, Scarlet slid out of the door and leant her back against the wall. Dry sobs of relief welled up in her throat and she ground her knuckles into her mouth. She pushed herself off the wall. She had to find Sinclair's father and her mother to break the news.

The next hours passed with aching slowness as they waited in the corridor for Sinclair to be disconnected from the ventilator and have exhaustive checks run on him. But he had crested the hill of recovery and all the news was good.

When they were allowed back into his room his eyes were closed again. But he must have heard their voices because he stirred and smiled at Scarlet.

'Did I dream you said you'd marry me?'

She rested her head on his chest. 'It wasn't a dream. I can't wait.' She kissed him gently on the lips and stepped back.

Sinclair smiled tiredly at his father. 'Hi, Dad.' He turned his eyes towards Scarlet. 'Have you met your new daughter-in-law-to-be?'

'And my new grandson. About time, too. Now, you get better soon, and I'll have a few more fine fellows like Cameron, thank you.'

Vivienne leant across and kissed Sinclair's brow. 'I'm just staying long enough to welcome you to the family. Take it easy, Sinclair, no new grandchildren yet,' she said, and stepped back.

Sinclair smiled up at her. 'And when do I get to welcome you into the family?'

Vivienne just smiled and said, 'We'll see.' The older couple slipped out.

Scarlet leant across and kissed his lips again. 'Thank you for coming back to us. We all love you. But I'm in love with you so don't go away again. Promise?'

'I promise,' he said, and his eyes closed.

EPILOGUE

THE bride wore a pale ivory gown that rustled as she walked and spring flowers nestled like a crown in her bright copper hair.

The marquee poles were satin-bowed and trailed with tiny white baby's breath that disappeared into the canopy. Most of the town seemed to have driven up the mountain for the ceremony and gaily dressed children played under the trees.

Frank McPherson stood tall and straight, his face creased with lines of happiness as he gave Scarlet away to his son. His eyes softened as he winked at the new woman in his own life and Vivienne, as matron of honour, smiled wickedly back at the man she'd been in love with all those years ago. The joy and love on the raised platform overflowed onto the gathered guests.

When the lone saxophonist played 'Ave Maria' the notes floated gloriously across the rolling green grass of the lookout and over the edge of the mountain. The vista below them stretched gloriously all the way to the sea as vows were taken and lives joined together for ever.

Cameron was perched in his old-fashioned pram, dressed in a miniature suit to match his father and grandfather. He clutched a satin pillow in front of him. As best man at his parents' wedding, he had a very important job to do.

Sinclair, tall and straight in his black suit, reached

across and untied one of the rings from the pillow. He dropped a kiss on his son's head before turning to his bride. Her eyes met his and for both of them the sun seemed to shine a beam right at them. He slid the ring onto Scarlet's finger and his voice carried strongly across the lawn.

'With this ring, I thee wed...'

Modern Romance™
...seduction and
passion guaranteed

Tender Romance™
...love affairs that
last a lifetime

Sensual Romance™
...sassy, sexy and
seductive

Blaze
...sultry days and
steamy nights

Medical Romance™
...medical drama on
the pulse

Historical Romance™
...rich, vivid and
passionate

27 new titles every month.

*With all kinds of Romance for
every kind of mood...*

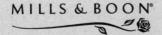

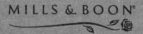

2 FREE

books and a surprise gift!

We would like to take this opportunity to thank you for reading this Mills & Boon® book by offering you the chance to take TWO more specially selected titles from the Medical Romance™ series absolutely FREE! We're also making this offer to introduce you to the benefits of the Reader Service™—

★ FREE home delivery
★ FREE gifts and competitions
★ FREE monthly Newsletter
★ Exclusive Reader Service discount
★ Books available before they're in the shops

Accepting these FREE books and gift places you under no obligation to buy, you may cancel at any time, even after receiving your free shipment. Simply complete your details below and return the entire page to the address below. *You don't even need a stamp!*

YES! Please send me 2 free Medical Romance books and a surprise gift. I understand that unless you hear from me, I will receive 4 superb new titles every month for just £2.55 each, postage and packing free. I am under no obligation to purchase any books and may cancel my subscription at any time. The free books and gift will be mine to keep in any case.

M2ZEA

Ms/Mrs/Miss/Mr ....Initials......................................

BLOCK CAPITALS PLEASE

Surname ....

Address ....

....

....Postcode.................................

Send this whole page to:
UK: FREEPOST CN81, Croydon, CR9 3WZ
EIRE: PO Box 4546, Kilcock, County Kildare (stamp required)